I0671102

EXISTENCE

By
Richard Mousseau

MOOSE HIDE BOOKS
imprint of
MOOSE ENTERPRISE PUBLISHING
PRINCE TOWNSHIP
ONTARIO, CANADA

cover illustration by Rick Mousseau

Existence
By Richard Mousseau
Copyright January 29, 2017.

Published January 2, 2019
by

MOOSE HIDE BOOKS
imprint of
MOOSE ENTERPRISE PUBLISHING
684 WALLS ROAD
PRINCE TOWNSHIP
ONTARIO, CANADA
P6A 6K4
web site www.moosehidebooks.com

NO VENTURE UNATTAINABLE

CREATED IN CANADA

Library and Archives Canada Cataloguing in Publication

Title: Existence / by Richard Mousseau.
Names: Mousseau, Richard, 1953- author.
Identifiers: Canadiana (print) 20189068884 | Canadiana (ebook)
20189068892 | ISBN 9781927393536
   (softcover) | ISBN 9781927393543 (PDF)
Classification: LCC PS8576.O977 E95 2019 | DDC C813/.54—dc23

EXISTENCE

Prologue

Life existed, though from a distance the observation would be difficult to believe or understand how existence survived. What once consisted as a human planet of social and scientific advancement, no longer inhabited the third planet from the fading sun. Swirls of blue tinges of vast oceans and various hues of white clouds had vanished within centuries of current knowledge of those beings inhabiting modern earth. For the creature standing on the rugged out-crop of a mountain, he had no knowledge of what the past world resembled. The vastness of brown coloured shades covering the landscape was all the man remembered since setting foot upon this locale. Forty-years of an accumulated age of sixty-five had been spent on the emptiness of this wasteland. A utopia for this armature archaeologist, filled with scenery of solitude and beauty that only he appreciated. At times, another cohabitant would complain about the loneliness of fellow human interactions, yet the woman had no desire to leave the tranquility of a home and wished to honour the legal bonding agreement with the man she had grown to love.

Having climbed out of the vent opening of rock slicing into the mountain, M12-12AT sat on a section of a petrified log he had fashioned into a seat. The climb out of the mountain was always an exhausting endurance test and filled with anxiety to bask in the open air and the warmth of the sunshine. On this day there was not much warmth delivered from the sun hidden behind grey clouds. This fourth quarter of the earth year brought cold winds casting snow streams off the retreating northern glacier. Glancing toward the distant wall of the glacier, he could not tell where the top edge ended, as if it blended into the thick clouded sky. A flow of air carried snow down from the top glacial edge, a waterfall flow of ice crystals gliding across the barren earth toward a small green oasis. By the end of the fourth seasonal quarter the land would be covered in wind-swept snow and the dark days of a never-ending first quarter winter. From this distance between the oasis and the mountain, the green of home seemed merely a dot on a desert of endless square kilometres. Home was the odd number of hectares of rejuvenating life and foliage.

Bundling up to retain heat, the rested man decided to advance towards home before a chill entered his body, and the cold of the night brought on by the advancing weather attacked. Darkness would shroud the landscape before reaching the warmth of home and an embrace by an accommodating woman. From the top of the mountain a vision of the vastness containing emptiness of vegetation, animals and humans often set the man into contemplating thought. The spring, summer, and fall seasonal quarters were quiet times, for only he and companion occupied the oasis. Now that the winter quarter was advancing, other humans would be making their travel paths towards the waiting comfort of individual buildings surrounding the main home and communal room. Off to the south a small cloud of dust interested the man's sight. A traveller was advancing, yet a day away. At this moment, the identity of the traveller was not known.

So much details of earth's history and the time-line of the rise and fall of mankind floated around in the man's thoughts, there was a lot of information that still needed to be acquired and understood. Today, he had acquired another clue. Patting the backpack as if to comfort the object inside, he hoped further clues of mankind's prehistoric history would be revealed, providing that its contents could be extracted. With animated gestures, of hands moving as if to explain thoughts being spoken in his head, the man lectured to the expanse that lay before emotional eyes. Light brown eyes that expressed warmth, highlighted the weathered face of short cropped beard hair. Matching grey of head hair randomly stuck out from beneath a knitted woollen toque. Though being in his early age of sixty full seasonal changes, a tall slim frame was bent and kinked from life's labour. Rising from a short rest on the petrified log seat, the man groaned as the body strained to straighten to a fully erect stance. His mind's thoughts began to vocalize and fade into the muted air absorbing the mist of warm breath beginning to chill.

"From the evolution of beings that became the first humans, they ventured over the land, harvesting the wild animals. Soon, knowledge occupied their thoughts and brain matter expanded. Humans clothed themselves and became agriculturists; built homes, towns, cities, towering structures, all the while amassing great armies for the sole purpose of destroying competing humans vying for existence, the pursuit of happiness and earth's riches. Ever expanding, humans advanced across the known world in search of knowledge and superiority. Great nations rose and fell under the guise of rule, religion and wealth. The continuous rape of limited substance of the earth demanded alternatives; elimination of the unwanted, exploration of the seas and the space above, then at the peak of superiority expectations of collapse occurred. Nations imploded, and human exodus became essential. No longer could the earth maintain stability. Why?"

Slightly twisting from side to side, the disillusioned man's arms extended with palms up, intent on accepting an answer of explanation from someone . . ., from the earth itself. No answer came forth.

"A void of informational history exists from the point of humanities' collapse and earth's rebellion against destruction by a self-induced destruction. The earth has burnt; the seas have risen and washed away the waste then advancing glaciers have cultivated the earth anew. How much time has passed; centuries, a millennium or longer? I . . . and those of us of kind that venture over the land and seas are mankind's remains of existence."

Dropping arms to his side, a sense of hope drained from a drawn face of sadness. A last scan of the vast landscape was taken as he turned to face all directions until stopping to face the direction of home. The sky began to turn a mixture of red, oranges with white winds of snow at the mountain's height. Taking a step forward, a last statement left the man's lips.

"This is existence!"

ONE

M12-12AT; is a designation given to a being created in the human nursery below the salt water seas that was the last inhabitable manmade refuge. Below the rising sea waters that swallowed what was left of accessible land, man had utilized submersible bubble habitats. Degradation of land and air prohibited humans from surviving as they once had. Seeking refuge beneath the waters allowed the privileged to survive and procreate in hopes of future generations to re-establish life on rejuvenating land. Time alone governed when and where humans would step upon terracotta. What human, animal, vegetation, insect, and single cell substance remained on the land surface when evolution's clock could not be advanced and setting it back in hopes of a reprieve could not be accomplished, would parish. No one could scientifically guess what manner of life would survive or if even the privileged below the ocean waters would emerge with future generations.

Being able to be self-sustaining in the multitude of ocean bubbles, mankind survived and created future generations of offspring. M12-12AT was a product of this desperate experiment to retain life on earth. Along with original inhabitants when the doomsday clock ran out, and every next generation throughout advancing centuries, humans managed to survive beneath the ocean. There they waited, and on every documented date would venture to the surface to judge when man could begin to venture upon the land once more. A generation before M12-12AT came into existence, occupants of the ocean people slowly began to send explorers and pioneers to establish land-based colonies. Advanced technological intelligent beings were in essence, cavemen upon the land using a mixture of the twenty-second century and fifteenth century technology to carve out a new world.

M12-12AT was a product of a barbaric infancy producing system. Though this system was required, it offended a natural family structure insisted upon since the first male and female humanoid decided to bond and care for an offspring. M12-12AT; is the male child to become known by the name of Mat, is a product generated to advance mankind's existence on earth. M = male, 12-12 = the twelfth generation after year one of the ocean bubble occupation, and the twelfth product of the host female incubation unit, A = blood type, T = the designation of the male sperm donor, a male possessing the qualification of a Teacher of life's information. Hopefully, Mat would inherit the qualities and intelligence of the male donor, acquire the ability to learn and in turn teach the current and next generations. Having a male donor of such qualities was the important ingredient and was strongly adhered to. Lest of importance, was the host female, though a fertile producer was very important. Intelligence and social qualities did not factor into the equation. A womb and the ability to gestate to term and ease of delivery held extreme importance.

Females of suitable structure were selected; hips of support and width of the birth cannel, breasts able to produce sustaining quantity and quality, and a reproductive system for multiple births in quick succession. Though not the norm, birthing mothers were of high importance for the continuation of the human race. Of those female children of inferior status were to become female drones; unable to produce children they would become workers of equal status to the males and perform as they saw fit. Female drones enjoyed the pleasures experienced by all humans, though gave up the essentials of becoming pregnant. No longer were their bodies suitable to produce, carry and deliver another human form. From time to time over the centuries beneath the oceans, the bubble female drones attempted to conceive and produce as their ancestors once did. Failure was inevitable with drastic loss of infants and female drones. Not one successful attempt occurred in the ocean bubble complex in one-hundred years. It seems that evolution played a hand within the confines of the ocean bubble population and augmented the female species to become infertile and structurally inadequate for reproduction.

The stock of birthing mothers had begun to dwindle by the time the ocean inhabitants began to resurface and venture upon the earth surface. Mat was a second-generation product to leave behind the ocean existence and become an earth person. Now in his sixties, he cannot remember seeing a human infant; its smell, cry, laughter and human interaction. Maybe when he was five-years old, there may have been a younger child. That was over fifty years ago when his own childhood was over and the teaching of the need to sustain human existence began. Absorption of all knowledge to survive needed to be learned. The basics of tool making, food gathering, and the cultivation of new vegetation required retained intelligence. Then a trade was selected, and that trade was learned and carried out throughout Mat's remaining existence in the outside world.

Sent to occupy the oasis at the tender age of twenty, Mat would sustain himself while exploring for the remains of the twenty-first centuries inhabitants, culture and technologies. This oasis was a prime location, inhabitable and at the edge of the receding glaciers. Earth, existing as a living, changing, entity had been in the process of rejuvenating itself. In a sense, the earth was healing by a purifying process. The twenty-first century birth of the ice age would freeze out the existence of disease and the menace of destructive inhabitants. In its path of growing and retreating, the high pressure of ice against earth would turn the soil; plough under the rumble of unwanted structures and return the earth to a rejuvenating rebirth.

Advancing from both poles, the encroaching ice forced humans and animals into a limited band of sustainable temperature within the band of the equator. Here the conflict to survive would be self destruction where only the purist would survive. Mankind has debated over the existence of time and well into the future about who will survive; be it the strong, the mindful, the religious, the political, the rebellious, the takers, the givers or the meek that shall inherit the earth. Space scientists have debated this very question when in need of selecting those few to be sent to inhabit a new colony on a distant planet or moon. To Mat's understanding as he endeavours to exist on this small oasis on the edge of known world, is that the common human shall triumph. A being of average intelligence that knows a little bit of knowledge about everything and is willing to learn a-new, learn to adapt, teach, share and cohabitate, will live on. When Mat reflects upon his mate and the few humans that return each winter to commune until spring, he wonders if existence will continue. Communications from the bubble community, or for that matter other settlements have not passed on word of the success of an infant population.

When the final minute of the doomsday clock advanced upon the hour, scientists announced the alarm bell to inform heads of states that it was time to leave earth. Preparations had been made for a mass transportation to the nearest pre-settled planet. Mat was not interested in that singular aspect of history, nor did he recall the name of the planet, or its location. Being a product of the ocean bubble population; he preferred to know of its history. Based on the line of thought of the earth-bound scientists, all agreed that the population should be an equal mix of all disciplines; scientific minded humans, technical, artistic and labour. All must be able to be adaptable to all disciplines. Unfortunately, when considering the stability of the future human population, undesirables were not included. Those that may hinder sustainability were discarded. Limited room was available within the various ocean bubble habitats constructed by individual territorial governments. Any person determined to have a handicap of physical or mental limitations, and those of criminal potential; the aged, religious or political persons with single-minded preference were all discarded. The masses were then left to fend for themselves through the self destruction of the earth.

What the ocean bubble community endeavoured to eliminate was anything that conflicted with the preservation of humanity and its continuation. By no means was the community prejudice towards the beliefs of an individual person in any manner of religion or political ideals; all were directed to keep those matters self-contained. Logic states that for the betterment of survival of the species, if distractions are kept out of the equation, there is a better chance of success. Race and skin colour; despite the efforts to overlook and not to take exception always seemed to be a cause of discontent from the beginning of time. The ocean bubble mandate was incorporated from the beginning of the inhabitation of the habitats; colour and race would not be a factor within the first generation of infants. All sperm and egg samples would be introduced with a genetic mix of all races and the fertilized egg implanted into birthing mothers. Without identification to birth mothers and fathers, infants were raised as brother and sister groups, thus eliminating a singular race identification. Skin colour became a mute factor and ethnic attributes once common was now diluted beyond singular identification. This was not the case for the space community or for the remainder of the population left on the earth surface to weather earth destruction and rebirth.

At the time that Mat was reaching the age of sixteen, troubles within the bubble communities were faltering because of a lack of birth mothers, and a rapid increase in population. Dispersion of inhabitants back upon the land insured a reduction of population within the bubble communities but did not guarantee a population increase among the new land settlers.

Mat had heard stories from the traveller, who had gathered information from encounters with decedents of those able to survive the dark years of mankind's down fall. Yet, stories are stories passed on, and variables of truth and fiction are blended into historical fact, or just stories for entertainment purposes. This was the traveller's objective to gather, retain and pass on to those wishing to know. Both Mat and mate were egger to hear of the latest year's gathered information from the traveller. From the mountain top, the traveller's slow-moving dust could be seen by Mat; maybe less than a day's distance away. Eagerness was not on Mat's side; the actual travel time may be two days.

For hours, Mat and Tell, traveller's acquired name, debated the down fall of mankind as humans were pushed towards the warmer climate as the ice age progressed. Tell was adamant that the first to become redundant were the weak, sick, aged, lazy, those intent on possessing political power, or religious superiority. When the value of money is gone, the rich flounder. The political no longer have support from the masses. Religion may save the soul and keep the mind at peace, in knowing that salvation is waiting in the afterlife, though, prayer will not feed the masses, nor protect from the evil, thus, religion and its leaders and followers fall. The crime minded; those that were intent on surviving on the greed of money, stealing, living off the worth of underlings, and were willing to kill and take what they wanted or needed by force lasted for a while. When there was nothing left to steel and the innocent killed, the criminal turned to killing each other. Soon, that aspect of society was gone for they did not know how to use the land, their mind or have physical ability to survive. The common man of physical ability and a mind of learning aptitude survived. By being scarce, living in solitude and avoiding the gathering of people in close quarters, they were surviving while cities, towns, villages and communes, of religious or cult or criminal, vanished.

After the traveller's last excursion, a year previously, he had brought news of an earth created space craft in complete content on the surface of a distant glacier. The intact craft was a transporter. This year there should be more news about the craft from an exploration crew. Mat waited with inquisitiveness about the craft's condition, content and reason for it being back on earth. Last year, Mat and the traveller discussed the possible success and possible failure of the space evacuation endeavour. What was on Tell's mind was, 'how did the destruction of mankind unfold?' This is when Mat pulled out a tattered book for discussion, a 'paperback novel' that he had found in the excavation area of the mountain.

Walking towards home on the flat expanse of short mossy ground covering, Mat recalled the conversation with Tell. What brought the subject to mind was the sudden gathering of goats noticing their owner heading for home. With the sky darkening, they knew it was time to go home, yet lingered until able to follow a protector home. Like their human counterpart, animals of all kinds perished, and some survived. It seemed that the predator animal, like their counterpart being the human criminal, dominated for awhile until prey became scarcer, then the predator vanished or dwindled to rare individuals. Huddling around Mat, the animals walked at a leisurely manner. Mat's thoughts drew to the science-fiction novel and Tell's bewildered glare.

"I tell you true, Tell," said Mat, his brown eyes wide with expression, while his short grey bearded face held no stimulation. "An air borne virus, a mutant common cold that tuned humans into flesh eating, deformed creatures. And, they only came out at night, because their eyes would burn in the sunlight."

"So, I take it they eat all the humans that did not have the virus?" Tell's thick pure white beard and thick head of hair hid the scepticism and childish interest in the possibilities. Attempting to shake his head from side to side, he felt hands on either side holding it still. "Eat all the humans until there was none?"

"Hold still Tell. Do you want me to cut your hair nice or just cut chunks out each time you move your head," scolded Kat.

Mat's mate, Kat waved scissors over Tell's seasonal growth of hair, its silky whiteness drifting effortlessly in the air of the domed building. Tall and slim with a strong build, Kat concentrated on the hair cutting. Just fifty-five years of age, she arrived at the oasis a year after Mat, to be the new agriculturist. New is not the proper designation, for there was no agriculturist here when Mat arrived. There were signs that someone had occupied the oasis; plants, animals, and well-kept buildings remained, but no keeper. This was before Tell's travels in this area, and the other returning winter occupants were also new. All that Mat could conclude was that the man, surely aged, must have perished beyond the oasis.

"Purely fictional," concluded Tell. "The story makes no sense. The mutants survive, yet eat every human, because they crave flesh and not healthy vegetables, and then they eat each other, so in conclusion, no one exists."

"Exactly, the fiction written by writers was so farfetched that it is ridiculous. A dying planet, and human being's attempt to exist is a horror story filled with truth. They should have been writing about the end of the world, and ways to survive. Maybe more people would have survived." Mat brushed fingers through his freshly cut hair in a manner of contemplation. "I guess these types of books are meant for entertainment?"

Holding his head stiff to prevent random clumps of hair being eliminated, Tell spoke with a slow drawl; only his light blue eyes danced with excitement. Framed by the white hair and matching beard, dusty brown skin showed the weathered results of his time travelling the expanse of the land. From the first day that he left the ocean bubble habitat at the age of eighteen, Tell had been assigned the task of collecting information from anyone encountered. Due to the lack of communication back to the ocean bubble, it seemed redundant to collect information; for what was the purpose of his task? Upon visiting the first and second person during his first venture, Tell realised the purpose and importance of his task. The exchange of dialogue, stories of adventure, details of survival and adaptations of farming, and plain gossip of everyday life was under the care of the traveller. From that first encounter, Tell gathered all information and freely delivered and catalogued for future references.

Enclosed in a tube-shaped enclosure supported on three paired tracks, the home slash transportation unit crawled at a snail's pace across the vast expanse of rejuvenated land. The curved surface of the tube structure and of the single pair tracked caboose provided the energy source for the drive mechanism. This old technology from the twenty-first century provided the solar electrical impulse to drive the track motors. This is an efficient and almost maintenance free power source, though the speed was equivalent to the rapid distance covered by a snail. Not only did Tell acquire and exchange information, the caboose gathered and delivered the exchange of products between inhabitants of each oasis.

Small encampments existed and were growing in number in the northern hemisphere over time as the earth heated and vegetation took root. Each year, new ocean bubble inhabitants that reached the maturity age between eighteen and twenty-five took their acquired knowledge and assumed the responsibility of inhabiting the new world. Success was based on the supply of births within the breeding program of the ocean bubble system. Evolution of women had declined over time; a fault of the breeding system. Only selected women of suitable condition became birthing vessels. Others became drone women assigned the same tasks as men; to go forth and inhabit the land and develop it. Encampments seemed sterile when viewed upon a first arrival; the land and animals were prospering but the human population was stagnant. Adults arriving from the ocean bubble were greeted with elation as if being first births. Tell had noticed that there was also a decline of new exports from the ocean habitat.

Travelling across his designated section of the northern area up to the receding glacier, the yearly trek encompassed established encampments and newly developing oases. Often, the distance between encampments was days and weeks of direct travel. Upon arriving for a first encounter with Mat, at the once abandoned oasis late one fall, Tell had decided to make this his yearly starting and returning point. Mat's oasis was the furthest oasis north and the closest one to the receding glacier. Several other parties had over time also decided to gather and make their winter habitation stay at Mat's oasis.

Both Mat and Kat expressed excitement when the winter season progressed. Soon Tell would arrive, then other returning wanders and maybe a newcomer. Though Mat and Kat enjoyed their cohabitation, they revelled in the accompaniment of others, sharing knowledge, stories and of most interest, gossip. Mostly gossip, for this was the intimacy that bonded humans. Mat and Kat provided plenty of gossip about each other to be delivered to distant inhabitants of the new world.

This single winter quarter, though dreary, seemed longer than others, yet passed too quickly when visitors departed. Mat knew that Tell was arriving; he would be the first, even a bit early. Knowing the pace of the slow-moving transport tube, he could not hold back anticipation to greet Tell. Mat had requested a bovine of any kind to add to the livestock. Maybe, Tell was able to acquire one. Over time the oasis menagerie grew; the goats were a healthy herd, chickens, ducks and geese flourished, and the fish pond fed by glacier water sustained a supply of fish. From research, Mat assumed the fish to be speckle trout; a tasty creature.

As the goats began to gather and follow Mat towards home, off to the side a lone donkey decided to take its place right behind Mat. Adhering to animal hierarchy, the goats trailed behind. At a time, Bud the donkey proved its worth by pulling a plough and packing on Mat's excursions, though now the old fellow was retired. Bud assumed the task of overseeing the goats and acting as guard. Predators had survived as did the grass feeders, though they were sparse, they did make an appearance now and then. Wojo, the resident dog, a Blood-hound of sorts was also retired and no longer ventured beyond the compound.

From a distance, Mat noticed that Wojo was laying down on the job. He lay with snout pointing in the direction of Tell's advancement. Despite reclining when on duty, the hound was aware of all surrounding activity. Bud snorted into the back of Mat's hand and at that instant

Wojo twitched a long ear, rolled to point a cold nose towards the advancing mixed herd.

Life was pleasing, and Mat enjoyed the work and the excavation study. Their cohabitation contract had expired some five complete seasons ago, for the second time. Mat was somewhat surprised that Kat stayed on being a bonding mate, and she never brought the subject up. Keeping his mouth shut, Mat never questioned her motives or reasons for the status quo. He was pleased with the current situation and enjoyed catering to Kat.

From a distance, the dome buildings blended coldly into the similar landscape, yet there was a warmth of belonging within. There was something missing, a sensation that Mat experienced when approaching at this point of two-hundred metres. It was an expectation of no-one greeting him with want and need. Wojo would greet with a raised paw and Mat would scratch and pull loose skin on its head. Kat was always affectionate. There was something else that was not there that should be.

When descending from the mountain before the glacier, he was excited and eager to arrive home. Then when approaching Bud and the goats, a different emotion between man and animal raised spirits. It was at that distance of two-hundred metres that a hollow feeling entered his chest and a disappointing empty emotion filled thoughts. When within the compound he shared a friendly greeting with Wojo and a loving emotion with Kat. In that two-hundred metre void a different love went unexpressed.

When the goats have kids and spend the day within the compound, Mat notices that he rushes across that two-hundred metre distance with excitement. There is a fulfillment of satisfied joy when reaching the goat nursery and picking up a kid to cuddle. For the duration of being at this oasis, he has never seen a human child. Has never seen the transition of a baby to a child to an adult, barely remembering his own development.

Mat often had considered sending a request back to the ocean bubble complex with a suggestion to send a child or two out to contract couples. At an oasis would allow growth, education, a trade and social interaction for both child and caregivers. As the years passed and age progressed, the urge to send a request dwindled. Anyway, what did he know about raising a child? Maybe if finding a book during an archive search that pertained to child rearing, he may have considered sending in a request. Because of the breading system developed by the ocean bubble directive, and knowing that drone women were sterile, he wondered if Kat experienced any maternal emotions. She would feed the goat kids and care for them but never handled them in front of Mat, as he did. When Mat had lingered behind a hay pile, he noticed that Kat would hug and rock a kid, providing that she felt secure that Mat was not observing.

A book was found today in useable condition but on a very different subject. Kat would be intrigued because it related to her agricultural interest and study. Emptiness within his chest passed when Mat bent to scratch Wojo behind the ears. While the flock of followers settled within the dome barn, Mat stared into the distance towards Tell's approach. The distance, flatness of land and surface curvature the cloud dust formed by the tube tracks could not be seen.

Tell's direction was from directly West. If Tell was a week early, then Mat expected the professors to arrive in about a week. The tree professors always came from the South. Upon arriving they would constantly complain about the cold, though relished the time to hibernate through the winter quarter. They had once made the mistake of staying south during a winter cycle and ended up teaching and working with settlers with no time to rest.

The professors were the wise men of philosophy, mathematics and literature, each dabbling in other trades. They were a necessity, for without their knowledge being passed along, mankind would be stagnant and living in the dark ages. Compared to living in the ocean bubbles or on a distant planet, surviving on the earth's terra-firma was living in the dark ages. Society would have to be created from the basics, and with knowledge, humans would be able to develop by using brain matter to manipulate the bounty of the earth. There existed a drastic extreme between basic existence and technology. Computers and devices of technology only existed within the ocean bubbles. There was no ability to mass produce electronics and they were useless on land where the hosting foundations did not exist. Intelligent humans were living a survival existence. Old world applications controlled by advance minded humans. Solar energy-powered track tubes were the only mechanical applications on the earth surface.

All three professors were old, and difficult to tell apart. Their long white beards and hair remained unkept, until Kat became disenchanted and trimmed them for a once a year clean up. Once clipped and brushed, individual features were revealed. Having resided for so long on travels within the long track tube, their mannerisms were interchangeable.

Like all current inhabitants and products of the ocean bubble birthing process, each person had an identification tag of letters and numbers. Identification names were subject to whim and anointed by others or adopted. When Mat had once inquired about the professor's acquired names, they produced a faded card of three men with names inscribed. They stated that they resembled the men when once being young, so adopted the names, 'Larry, Moe and Shemp'. Neither of the professors knew what the word 'Stooges' meant.

Like the professors' ability to provide education, the book Mat had retrieved from the excavation, a complete history of society from the twenty-first century was waiting to be discovered. Maybe he would discover more about the 'Stooges'.

On Tell's previous year's visit, news was delivered that Doc would not be arriving. Word was that Doc had disappeared without a trace. Mat turned to see Kat digging up the remainder of the fall harvest. The thought of having no doctor making rounds was a worry. What if Kat took sick, what would he do? Doc was a loner and declined travelling with the professors, despite their concern about the man's age.

Kat's full figure and solid structure did not hint at poor health. This concern was Mat's manifestation of being left along, after-all, Kat had never renewed the cohabitation contract. Turning, Kat's short brown hair caught the cool breeze and fluttered about rosy cheeks. A smile grew as her eyes fixated on Mat approaching. Knowing Mat always found a trinket to bring back for her, a giddy excitement sparkled in green eyes. Brown skin pigments flushed.

"Hello, Mat."

"Afternoon Kat. How was your day?"

"Just fine." Leaning, she peeked at the small pack that Mat carried on a shoulder. The small pack should be empty, for Mat's meals should have been devoured. "Your pack looks the same size it was this morning. Did you not like the meals?"

"Oh, yes, devoured every last crumb. I did not share a morsel with a very hungry mole mouse that begged," Mat explained, teasing Kat by not presenting the find to her.

"Do I have to beg for my gift?"

"Well!" Mat slowly withdrew the pack. Pretending it was heavy, lowered it to the ground to open.

"What is it, not one of those useless gold things again?"

"Heck no, I am never going to tote gold again, useless artifacts." Withdrawing the oversized book, he presented it to her.

Kat's eyes widened for the thick book looked heavier than the golden sculpture. Brushing off the film of dirt, she read, "Jamie Oliver's international cook book with everyday easy recipes."

"You're a great cook," Mat interjected, worried that the intention of the gift had other undertones. "It's a resource book, to study the foods and eating habits of the twenty-first century humans."

"Don't be silly, it is a great gift. I am tired of cooking the same thing over and over. You are a good cook too, but something different would be exciting." Kat flipped the pages to study the well-preserved pictures, suddenly excited to try one.

"If we are start with the first recipe, we'll never have a repeat for years."

"Tonight, it is just stew," Kat added.

Mat hid a smirk of disappointment. "From the mountain I saw trail dust coming from the West. Tell should be here in a day or two," Mat said turning to point.

Before turning back to Kat, she was gone. Greens bounced out of the sack she carried as excited feet hopped towards the house dome. Eyes darted to each new page flipped.

"Kat?"

"Super is ready, I am going to find a recipe to surprise Tell with."

Bending, Mat picked up greens on Kat's trail toward the dome house. Wojo dragged a lazy hind end into motion and followed.

TWO

Tell's head bounced against the seat cushion forcing eyes to open. He tried to determine how long he had dozed? Through the dirt film on the tube's front window, he observed the declining day light. 'Another day of travel,' he thought to himself, calculating the time it would take to reach Mat and Kat's place. Though he had travelled the same route once a year for the past . . ., too many years, the ever-shifting sand continuously eradicated any fixed trail. He would have to guess direction based on visual references of the glacial location and the arcing sun. A better position would be gathered from star readings at night, providing that the skies were clear. With the approach of the winter quarter, less and less of the heavens could be seen. Knowing he was a week early, he doubted that Mat had raised the light beacon for guidance.

The twenty-foot tube was basically a large solar motor consisting of a solar skin and storage batteries under the floor. Though slow moving at a crawl, the tube was structurally strong and enduring. Minimal light was required to maintain battery charge. If power was too low, the tube would automatically stop to rejuvenate. At one time, Tell would step out and explore until the tube started to move again. At an easy jog he could overtake the creeping machine and board. The last time this situation occurred, Tell struggled to catch up. In that moment he realized that age was taking its toll on his body. During this seasonal travel, Tell contemplated settling in one place. Settle?

This tube; a roving accommodation and transporter was the only advanced technology on the regenerating earth surface. From what knowledge of the previous history of mankind he had accumulated, mankind was mentally advanced yet survived in a prehistoric world. The modern world of the twentieth and twenty-first century had collapsed. Mankind sought refuge on distant planets and in the submerged floating ocean colonies while the earth convulsed. The earth's magnetic poles shifted and created eight multiple poles. Weather and climate advanced in heat then retreated to a new ice age. As a farmer would plow and till the soil, glaciers had cultivated ninety percent of the earth's land mass.

Thousands of earth years had passed before man was forced to leave the over-crowded and sustenance failing habitats of the ocean colonies and attempt to exist on the birthing land. Tell had a difficult time visualizing what the modern world of the twenty-first century was like. Remnants did exist in the ocean habitats; computers, radios, and electronics. Those limited products only worked within the habitat. None worked on the earth's surface, and satellites that once circled the earth in a space orbit no longer existed. Tell had once found remnants of a satellite during travels.

Dangling from a chain above his seat a simple round ancient compass hung, a gift from Mat. Due to the earth's multiple magnetic poles, the simple dial continuously spun. A simple guidance indicator was now useless. Glimpsing past the compass through the window, Tell focussed on the tube's forward shadow caused by the west setting sun. He pulled a track leaver until the snail advancing tube lined up with the shadow, a course correction. If it had been possible to communicate with Mat, Tell would have given notice of an early arrival. Mat would then have raised the guidance beacon for Tell's guidance.

Under the darkness of the outside world, Tell caught a glimpse of his reflection in the window along with the inside of the long empty tube. "Kat will have a field-day with this hair and beard. Dam, it's white!" Tell tilted head from side to side and up and down to inspect. Hair was too long and hanging over brows. Lips could not be seen behind whiskers. He was tired of brushing back whiskers when eating. Thinking of food, he turned to face the kitchen area and contemplated what meal he would make. It was his turn to create something palatable. Last night's meal was filling, though lacked the finesse of seasoning and presentation.

These past three seasonal quarters was the first and only time that he shared the tube with another human being. The cohabitation was strange, enjoyable, complex and bewildering. He could not understand why he never requested cohabitation during the forty seasonal quarters of his age of sixty-eight. Standing, Tell felt a twitch in a knee, the leg forgetting to wake up with the rest of the body. At the kitchen, he closed eyes and reached randomly between a row of loose pages. Selecting a sheet of paper, he withdrew one of Kat's recipes. Nodding, lips smiled behind the cloak of whiskers. "A tasty recipe."

Always aware of the tube's movement, Tell adjusted his stance when a clank was heard against the tube's front V blade. A left track raised a bit as it climbed over an obstacle. The trailer tube's tow-bar clanked. Inside of the tube trailer, the lone livestock passenger braced itself against the curved wall as the trailer's left track climbed over the obstacle. The bovine seemed calm, as if the female had spent an entire life in such a machine.

Leaning against the bovine's extended belly, Sally moved the round end of a stethoscope searching among the guttural sounds. "There it is," she said in a general manner. The bovine's ears twisted back towards the attendant's voice. "Nice and strong." A bright smile forced grayish warm skin to beam with delight. Moving to the other side, Sally repeated sound testing. When a strong sound was detected, her smile grew.

Long braids of reddish hair flopped onto shoulders when Sally stood erect. Not heavy nor light, she stood solid with no noticeable curvature of body. From shoulders to hips the body held the same form, and she moved with grace, not what would be expected for a working veterinarian.

"You are having twins," Sally said, her voice as delicate as her movements. "You are doing fine. Once we reach the oasis, you will have time to rest before delivery. And, I will be there for your first delivery."

Stationed at a southern oasis as a second vet, Sally was concerned about the welfare of the bovine on such a long journey. The mystery of the man behind the white hair and beard also interested Sally's adventurous intent. At fifty-five quarter seasons, she felt in need of a change. When Tell approached the owner of the bovine on Mat's behalf, Sally stepped forward. She did not wait for a personal introduction, though knowing who Tell the traveller was.

"This bovine comes from fine stock. Our breeding program has been successful," Sally's light voice danced on air peeking Tell's attention. "We believe the domesticated breed bred in the wild with the last roaming bison. Nomadic bison able to forage on meager sustenance and withstand the global cooling."

Tell listened, teased by the lilting voice, though unconcerned about the animal's heredity. He was just the messenger and transporter.

"As you can see, this female is short legged, stout and has a good long hair coat, ideal for northern conditions. How far are you taking this female?" asked Sally, brushing hair from the bovine's eyes.

Startled, Tell's eyes widened. He did not know what he was getting into, and Mat did not specify, or had he. He stuttered, "Far . . ., to Mat and Kat's oasis."

"I met Mat once. Does he plan to bread? Is there a male available? For the bovine, I mean. If not, I recommend artificial insemination. I'll get a kit ready for . . .," Sally hesitated for only a moment, not even enough time for Tell to reply to a first question. "You do know that this bovine is pregnant, due in the fourth quarter. I should accompany you and take care of it for a healthy delivery. A healthy offspring would be a bonus for Mat and Kat. You do travel alone, I know by your reputation. Do you know what would be best?"

Tell managed a slight sway of the head yet was still confused in thought about a male bovine. He knew Mat and Kat had a variety of livestock, though he never paid much attention to details.

"Would you allow me to accompany the bovine? Better still, would you be interested in a cohabitation contract, limited of course for the duration of travel time and delivery of a calf. That is just details, don't worry about that. I have an unused cohabitation contract with my gear."

Handing over a lead rope, Sally wiped a hand on a pant leg then extended it to shake Tell's hand.

"Nice to meet you Tell, my name is Sally."

"Sally," Tell whispered in response.

"By the time you and the stock-man load up the bovine, I'll be back with gear and the cohabitation contract."

In a blink of an eye, Sally vanished leaving a bewildered man eyeing the rope leading to the wide eyes of an amused bovine. The stock-man leaned against the hairy creature, his humorous grin catching Tell's questioning stare.

"Tell," said the stock-man. "you've got a good deal here, a pregnant bovine and a vet to take care of it." His hand patted the dusty coat of the bovine. A last comment was of praise, "Sally has had that blank cohabitation contract for . . ., since she showed up here as a kid."

Befuddled, Tell did not know what to think, or say. Maybe it was age that allowed him to just accept what unfolds. By the time the bovine was loaded, Sally had stowed personal gear into the main drive tube then brought veterinary gear into the tube trailer. While she checked conditions and the bovine, Tell closed up and walked forward to the drive tube, a hand scratching through frizzed white hair.

That was a quarter season ago, and their cohabitation had been mutual. The cohabitation contract had been signed, though the duration section had been left blank. Tell was confused as to why Sally had pined the contract at the side door. She mentioned that there was no better place; because all decisions of importance are made either when exiting or entering.

Stepping down from the trailer tube, Sally jogged ahead to grasp the drive tube's railing. Entering, warm hazel eyes glanced at the cohabitation contract. It was unchanged, indicating the status was still mutually acceptable. The aroma of spiced food and the sight of Tell happily cooking brought a wide smile to Sally's face.

"Almost ready," said Tell, his exterior blank expression smiling under the expanding beard.

THREE

There is a certain smell that permeates in and around the housing of animals. It is a combined smell yet can be individualized by animal type. A warm aroma filled the domed barn. Bud had laid down to rest skinny, tired legs, its sweet smell of grass breath mingled with the rub grass aroma on its hide. A good afternoon roll and back-scratch gave its coat of fall hair a fresh perfume smell. That smell being far from the low-end scale of the goat aroma of acidic urine smell of the male goat. Even the female goats emitted a pheromone smell during the rut season. Wojo had taken in a long sniff when entering the dome. In that one whiff, all domestic animals were accounted for and grouped in their sections of the barn. Satisfied that all was normal, the old hound dropped to its side at the entrance.

Having accomplished the feeding and bedding down of stock, Mat exited the barn into the dark of the night. Glancing to the centre of the compound where the tethered beacon light was housed, he contemplated the necessity of raising it into the sky. Tell was only a day or so distance away and should be arriving during daylight hours. There was a slim chance that Tell would miss the oasis. Mat did not sense any formation of inclement weather or storms. In thought, Mat decided to raise the beacon light tomorrow as a precaution. The professors would be arriving within a week as per their usual schedule. Maybe they considered arriving early as Tell had done. Was there some reason for Tell's early arrival? Regardless, the light beacon would be raised tomorrow.

Turning his head towards the resident dome, Mat sniffed an odd smell, not hideous, rather pungently sweet. Twisting the head towards the barn opening, there was a wall of animal smells wafting to meet the tasteful aroma from the resident dome. Crossing the centre compound and letting his nose lead the way, Mat opened the resident door. A full blast of warm air greeted him, dousing all senses with euphoric aromas.

"Definitely different?" said Mat to Kat at the cooking counter. He noticed the open cook book on the counter.

"Very interesting!" replied Kat, a hand shaking a spice container over a pot.

The cook book from thousands of years before their current existence brought curiosity and an adventurous interest in preparing food. During the ocean inhabitation, the growth of food products and consumption was based on the ocean's ability to sustain and provide.

Having existed on the earth after the glaciers began to recede, there was a need to adapt and learn to consume earth provided products. Lost was the culinary preparation. Jamie Oliver's cook book from a prehistoric time opened the world of creativity for Kat. Mat would be the first to taste-test. At this moment, Mat had no objection, based on the tantalizing and teasing aromas. A bit too eager, Mat rushed through cleaning up in a haste to sit at the table. Placing servings on the table, Kat noticed Mat's uncombed hair.

"Hungry, are you?"

Not giving pre-evaluation of the meal, Mat nodded slightly. "It has been a long day." Lips pressed together as the corners gently curved up into a diminutive smile.

Kat's eyes twinkled internally with delight, thoughts questioning why she liked the man even before meeting him. She attempted to calculate the number of quarter seasons that had passed since first arriving? It was a while ago. A chance conversation with the three professors at an Eastern ocean coastal departure compound intrigued Kat's mind.

Pressed for time, the professors were eager to travel and reach Mat's oasis before winds brought northern snows. Less than an afternoon of conversation was offered to Kat before departure. In a haste for more details of inland life, she requested permission to travel with the professors. Unaccustomed to having anyone travelling with them, the professors were skeptical of having a potential burden. As per their ways, the professors conferenced while Kat stood peering on from a distance.

Kat's short brown hair was teased by the light ocean breeze as greenish eyes darted about the commotion of the compound. She was nervous and agitated to have stepped onto land for the first time as a young female person. Without looking, she knew that landers were staring at her pinkish skin, an effect of longevity within the ocean habitats. A lack of natural exposure to weather gave oceaners a pinkish colour, regardless of underlying tones.

"Upon first observations, I notice that this oceaner is not of meek build," Pie began to say as teeth ripped a bite-size chunk of dried meat from a tube. "Not under-fed, stout, and of sturdy build."

Phil eyed the slim frame of his associate, his own taste buds wanting a taste of the tube meat. His mind overruled the craving that a short, plump body desired. "Unlike you, my good friend, we sturdy creatures of shortness and bulk are suitable to survival on the barren lands."

"I am also short," Story added, his hands gesturing to a skinny frame and drawn features. "I do think it is your cooking that is starving professor Pie and myself."

"Then why am I gaining girth when just watching professor Pie eating?" Phil stared at the smiling lips of professor Pie. "See, I gained a pound."

Reaching into a pocket on the inside of a draping coat, Story retrieved a grain ball and secretly popped it into his mouth. "The question at hand is, of what purpose has young Kat in mind? She has no placement, no cohabitation contract, and has only asked us of what we have seen. I dare say, her mind is curious."

"We cannot allow just anyone to tag along indefinitely," Pie stated, avoiding eye contact with Phil. Out of courtesy, he put the tube meat behind his back. "Does she have a trade, a calling, any landers experience?"

Listening with intent, Kat felt that the professors were intent on finding reasons to deny her request. She would have to find a purpose in her favour that would please the professors. A bold statement was needed. "You are professors, are you not? Professors teach, and answer questions from those in need and of the curious. I am curious and have many questions."

Pretending not to hear Kat's words, the professors bunched with backs turned towards Kat. For a moment with their minds filled with the combined knowledge of math, engineering, philosophy, science, literature and history, they were unable to counter the statement. Eyes rolled, white beards twitched, and thumbs twirled above hands clasped in front of their similar draped coats.

"It is our calling to teach," Pie confirmed, straightening with pride.

"We are not a transporter of human cargo," countered Phil, his pudgy cheeks giggling as air puffed in and out through parted lips. "It is my turn to cook tonight and I plan to make . . .,"

"We know it is, why do you think I've been chewing on dried meat?" Pie rocked on toes and heels. "And Story has also been sneaking grain balls."

"Professor Story, how could you? I am making grain ball soup." Phil swayed a bald head from side to side in disappointment. "You will spoil your appetite."

With head turned slightly away, Story popped another grain ball into his mouth. "The thought of every meal on a third rotation spoils my appetite. I, a skinny short man is the most disadvantaged amongst the three of us."

"Will there be a side dish of meat with the soup?" Pie questioned, in a tone that resembled a demand.

"No."

"Bread, biscuits, maybe cake?" hinted Story.

"No."

"No!" Pie and Story jointly harmonized.

"No!"

"I am a horticulturist by education and wish to put myself into the trade. And, I must add . . ., that I exceed in the preparation of all consumable agricultural products."

There remained silence among the professors. Kat inched forward in anticipation of a quick answer, yet the professors continued to ponder.

"I also took a second educational specific in culinary preparation of all food types."

Still, the professors stood silent, as if being too smart in their own educational disciplines to understand what Kat was saying.

"I can cook, and cook well in the preparation of meats, vegetables, grains and wild organics. I will do all the cooking for you." Kat leaned forward with hands interlocked and pressed in tension.

"Sounds good to me," Pie instantly whispered to the professors.

"No complaint here," Story added.

Phil held out, hesitated to agree. "She must give us a destination to depart. Our acceptance of a passenger cannot, must not and will not be permanent. And, she starts as fulltime cook tonight."

In unison all whispered confirmation, "Agree."

Their smiling grins faded when turning around to face Kat. Pie and Story, standing on either side of Phil, gently elbowed the man to take charge and inform Kat of intentions, duration and end result.

"Kat," Phil began, his chin and jowls resting forward and on neck flab. "Our destination is the furthest northern oasis inhabited by Mat, he is an archeologist and raises assorted livestock. He is a suitable man and has cultivated the land and has crops." Patting hands against a protruding belly, he edged closer to a finality. "We will take you there, and you must depart from us and our tube transporter. Once there you are on your own to decide circumstances.

With an affirmative nod, Kat accepted. In turn each professor nodded, smiling and giddy with excitement on the inside. Exterior expressions prevailed. Pie pointed to their tube beside a stocking dome.

"That is our transporter tube. You may store your gear and . . ., if you please . . ., for we are about to depart . . ., you may acquaint yourself with the interior and functioning appliances . . ., if you are so inclined . . ., without persuaded pressure from us . . ., individually or as a combined entity. . .,"

"Forgive Pie's rambling lips and distorted mind," Story said interrupting. "Start cooking an evening meal . . ., go . . ., hurry."

"Thank you . . ., thank you," Kat said, instantly skipping towards the professors' transportation tube.

"Thanks Story," Pie said, tension draining from his form. "We do not have to cook . . ., at all, for the entire trip."

"No more of Phil's cooking," added Story.

"Thank goodness," exclaimed Phil, his bulk shaking as if discarding unwanted pressure. "I hate my own cooking."

"And we suffered." Pie snickered.

"On purpose, you made us eat your bland, watery soup, on purpose." Story's head swayed in disappointment.

"I took my turn, did my duty."

"Tonight, a real meal, a tasty meal." Story popped a grain ball into his mouth.

"If she really can cook, she may have deceived us," Phil's voice had turned cold with confliction.

"Why did you say that?" Pie's face cringed.

"Phil, you are always on the side of fault. What kind of philosopher are you?" scolded Story.

Conflicted and dumbfounded, the professors stood in place until Kat entered the tube, and in place they waited until she called them to come to the evening meal.

The professors were a bit spoiled during the trip to Mat's oasis. Never had they had, or in the future have such nourishing and well-presented meals by Kat. They noticed the exchange of eye contact and greeting mannerisms between Mat and Kat and knew that their cook would not be returning with them in the spring quarter season. It was after a third night of an out-door walk that Kat presented a cohabitation contract. Mat now relished the meals that the professors would only savour during the winter seasonal quarter.

31

Mat lifted the lid of a pot and was attacked by the seasoned aroma of the dish. "That Jamie Oliver recipe has come to life by your amazing talent." Mat was no fool and knew where to place due credit.

Smiling, Kat hovered, her eyes riveted on Mat's face to detect tell-tale signs of approval or disapproval. Without revealing the tingling sensation of satisfaction of Mat's approval, she sat. a blush of emotion tinted her face of pinkish grey skin.

FOUR

Though the professors were of drastic differences of height and weight, they dressed in a similar draped coat, a short frock to depict their trade. From an early age they gravitated together, while each pursued different educational path. Pie pursued math and engineering; Phil progressed with philosophy and science; Story excelled in literature and history.

Having spent their youth enjoying the other's company and freedom to argue, discuss, agree and disagree, their bond never faltered. When age and demand for information by landers required them to leave the ocean habitat, the three professors jointly left together. There was no discussion and no pre-planning, they exited the ocean habitat, stored their gear in the same tube transporter and ventured forth to deliver education.

Their departure was not as simple as one would expect. Being minds of higher education also limited the professor's ability to understand simple logic at times. Upon stowing gear within the tube transporter, they sat and commenced a discussion about which discipline of knowledge would be most important to landers. There they sat, discussing while the transporter's electric motors hummed, eager to distribute torque to the drive train.

"Do you realize professors," Pie began to say, interrupting Story's description of lost dialects. "it has been hours since I have devoured any nourishment."

Phil took sight of the slim, tall, seemingly under-fed man. "You have devoured three kelp biscuits within the last . . ., how long have we been here?"

"We are not moving!" Story leaned to glance at the forward drive station, the mess area and the open door. "Should there be a driver, a cook and someone to provide destination instructions?"

"All important," Pie agreed. "though a cook would be most prudent, because my stomach is growling."

Having stated immediate facts, they did not act upon them, rather continuing to discuss educational topics. Light streams advanced across the front window then began to subside into the dimness of evening. While arguing about the importance of history, the professors began to hear a strange sound at the door.

Concerned about the length of time the tube transporter remained stationary, the compound's manager stuck her head into the tube to gain the occupants' attention. "Professors . . ., Professors . . ., is there a reason for remaining?"

Pie turned his thin face dappled with a growing beard. "Yes, hello. Are you our cook? I am famished."

"By chance our driver?" asked Story. His short thin frame a miniature representation of Pie seemed to be childish in stature.

Even at a young age of twenty seasonal quarters, the professors presented the maturity of their elders. They were also hindered by a lack of everyday skills and experience of life on land. Of the three, Phil showed the advancement of balding, though his beard was more advanced than the others.

"It is possible," suggested Phil. "that our visitor is both cook and driver, just arriving with our destination instructions." He patted a plump belly with self praise.

A distressed glare of narrowing eyes and contorted facial muscles expressed frustration. Stepping into the tube, the compound manager was ready to admonish the simplistic minds of the professors. With restraint she held back, feeling compassion for the men when seeing their innocent faces.

"Did you attend the orientation classes?" she asked, a voice soft yet direct.

Heads nodded, "Yes."

"Did you pay attention to the instructor discussing operational factors of the transportation tube? The functions of the tube interior and appliance applications, and food preparation and storage? Also, the instructional data of travelling to various locations? And, what your responsibilities are?"

The professors nodded.

"Absolutely, everything pertaining to our ability to teach our subjects and answer any question on any subject," Phil proudly answered.

Pie beamed a cocky smile. "We are professors of education, and I can assure you that we listened and understood everything pertaining to education."

A bewildered thought seemed to be answered in the manager's mind. Still, she had to ask, "What about the first part of my question?"

Story was ready to answer, feeling cocky about having the right answer. "Yes, I listened, though it was of no importance to us. I do trust that the drivers, mechanics, cooks and topographical map readers were paying attention. After all, that is their trades."

Slowly the manager's head slumped with disappointment. She would now have to be blunt and tell the three men that they should have listened, for they were now on their own. At the same moment there was sympathy towards the men for being so inept.

"You should have listened," her voice was clear, firm, yet soft. "You are on your own; you must cook for yourselves, operate and drive this transportation tube, determine destinations and plot courses. Having not listened and paid attention during training, it is now left up to you to read all manuals and be on your way."

Blank faces of the professors stared at the compound manager until the meaning of what was said registered in their minds. Heads turned to each other for answers. No one volunteered a response.

"Really . . ., no response, no clue within your minds filled with learned knowledge. I am blessed to be a person of average mentality and an inquisitive mind." Taking a deep breath, she pointed to a compartment. "All manuals are there in that compartment labelled manuals. I suggest you read, learn and have this tube transporter moving out of the compound before I leave in a half hour."

Closing eyes, the compound manager was able to block the expressions of the professors. With agitation, she hurriedly escaped before a multitude of questions could be directed towards her impatient mind. Slumping, each professor contemplated thoughts, for logically they should be able to read and understand the manuals then put actions into logical applications. The forced closing of the tube door awakened the attention of the professors. Heads turned towards the sound, their eyes wide awake to this new reality.

Story stood with authority, eager to take charge. "Being a professor of literature, able to speed read and retain facts, and instantly comprehend at an above average speed, I shall read the manuals aloud. Pie, man the controls of this transporter."

"I shall, I am a professor of engineering, and the physical application cannot be difficult." With hands resting in coat pockets, Pie approached the controls, resisting the need to place hands to the task.

"What shall I do?" Phil inquired.

"Are you not a professor of science?" stated Story.

"Yes!"

"Cook, I'm hungry," Pie's voice echoed from the front of the tube.

"A sub section of science is experimental compound mixing, heating and cooling." Story lifted a manual for appliance operations.

"Cooking is basically the mixing of elements, adding spices and heating."

"I have studied theoretical science," Phil implied.

Sitting onto the pilot seat and with a sensation of power and pride, Pie raised his voice, "I'm the driver, Story is the manual reader, so that leaves you to be the cook."

As Phil approached the preparation area, Story passed eyes over two manuals open on a counter. Discarding unimportant sentences, he read aloud giving directional instructions to Pie and Phil simultaneously. "Pie, push lever 'forward motion' into notch one. Phil, turn righthand control on heat appliance to first notch."

A glow of red showed on the glass surface of the heat exchanger just as the forward motion of the tube was felt.

"We have motion," exclaimed Pie, slightly eager to push the lever to the second notch.

"Fill pot with water from the blue tube above drain basin." Story turned his head from left to right so that instructions would be delivered to and accepted by the correct person. "During night travel leave lever in notch one. Midday travel may be set to notch three."

Pie withdrew his hand from touching the lever. Disappointment showed on an excited face. Phil held the water-filled pot in mid air waiting for further instructions.

"Levers indicating lights, move to night position. Place pot on heating surface. Empty soup mix into water." Story's eyes scanned the manual page, knowing that Phil was in need of finding the soup mixture. "Dried soup mixture retrieved from the dried storage dispenser, left and above cooling department. Interior light lever located on interior control panel."

As directed, Phil retrieved the soup mix as the interior lights brightened the interior of the tube. A simultaneous smile formed on each face after their initial success. Pie's smile drained when looking out through the window. Far ahead, the compound road led out onto the vast landscape. At such a slow speed, Pie would have plenty of time to correct direction away from sloping banks and maintain a passage on the road. Lack of experience dictated otherwise.

"Story!" Pie's voice gurgled. "Course correction needed."

Story's eyes darted from the window to the manual, his fingers searching for instructions. "Levers on arms of chair used to correct course. Left lever – left direction, right lever – right direction. Use individually or in tandem. Do not use both in forward or reverse motion. Levers must be used in opposing direction."

"Why?" asked Pie.

"Just don't," Story argued the point.

Pulling back on the left lever, the transporter's right track advanced beyond the locked left track and made a course correction.

Releasing the lever, Pie relaxed in the seat. Lifting hands off the levers, they were folded comfortably across his chest. "No problem. All is well."

"Soup is boiling. How long must it boil until ready?" Phil asked, his head hovering over the pot and nose inhaling the aroma.

"I'm hungry," came Pie's frequent demand.

Thus, began the professors' journey across the landscape bringing their educational knowledge to inhabitants of small villages and occupied oasis. By chance, the professors arrived at Mat's location before the winter quarter. At about the same time Tell had arrived. Finding the reclusiveness and companionship of the gathering suitable, a winter repose became a habit. Not much had changed for the professors, other than age and appearance. Pie maintained a tall slim figure with a long straight white beard and full head of straight hair. Story remained skinny and short, as if the once young man forgot to grow. Pride of appearance was maintained with a short white beard and head of hair. It was Phil that contradicted skinny associates, his plump, short body was highlighted by a bushy white beard and a bald head.

Heading northward, the professors were eager to arrive at Mat's oasis. Having travelled to the same northern destination, they relied on the light beacon to guide their arrival. Efficiency of map and topographical reading was still a hindrance throughout these many seasonal quarters. They were anxious to greet Mat, Kat and Tell. Eager to introduce their new companion, Professor Art.

Slightly younger, Professor Art was an equal and of the same mannerisms and complexities. He was suited to be among them, and them to him. A chance meeting during travels and during an endless marathon of intellectual discussion, they realized that they had travelled a great distance. Unable to rectify or reverse the situation, they accepted the fact and continued as a foursome.

Professor Art wore the same attire as all professors, a short-draped coat, though his beard and hair was just in the process of turning white. Slightly taller than Story, and fit, he was considered an average man. Like Story, he kept hair and beard trimmed and neat. Art's education did not clash with the professors. Art possessed the study of the arts of painting, sculpture, games and athletic fitness.

Not knowing their exact location, the professors were aware that they were heading in a north-west direction. Northern winds brought the coolness of snows from receding glaciers. Constantly, they stared into the distant horizon in search of Mat's light beacon. Only coloured streams of vertical lights illuminated the distant sky. Northern lights danced in shimmering colours in the thin cold air.

FIVE

Human-kind had survived through the dark ages of the advancing ice-age. The most successful groups were the ocean inhabitants. Retaining the ability to learn and advance, they adapted an existence on the floating habitats; progressed in education; adaptation of ocean food sources and propagation by means of a breeding program. Habitats created by all previous earth nations adopted the same breeding program. Over time distinct skin colour mutated into a spectrum of brown and grey colours; even two-tone and dapple pigmentation developed. Those features of race identifications from the twenty-first century were mixed randomly through each generation. Exchanges of donor sperm and eggs between the scattered ocean habitats created a single ocean species.

At a time during the advancing heating of the earth, climate change physically killed inhabitants in the equatorial band of the earth. Migrating humans sought the cooler ranges of the Arctic and Antarctic zones. Limited land mass remained for suitable habitation. Rising oceans swallowed the landscape. Humans and animals of all species fought to survive. Humans clinging to the land were unable to adapt or compete agriculturally or as predators. Mammal carnivores succeeded, mammal herbivores survived, reptiles, birds, and insects survived by consuming vegetation and devouring humans.

When the earth began to cool, what humans and wildlife remaining migrated back to the equatorial zone in advance of polar glaciers. Earth bound humans digressed to a caveman existence of survival and a reduced mentality developed. In contrast, the ocean inhabitants advanced and survived while maintaining a peek population. The rising oceans enhanced an abundance of growth. Though maintaining and expanding ocean habitations, some abilities of the twenty-first century were lost. Communications globally no longer existed. The earth's magnetic fields changed and created havoc. Satellites no longer existed.

Industry was limited to what could be produced on ocean platforms. Oil and gas production was limited to individual ocean habitats. Ships no longer existed. They floated freely for awhile until nature's whims toyed with them until destruction. Those humans clinging to their structures succumbed to the same fate. Solar conversion and ocean turbines became the basics of power, industry creation and study.

History lessons did not dwell on the migration of humans into space during the late twenty-first century. Once the transporter ships left for a distant habitational planet, contact ceased. During the death and rebirth of the earth over these thousands of years, ex-earth patriots have not returned.

Survival of the newly developed human species became a priority on ocean habitats. By mutual-agreement, limitations were an enforced must. Emotions, a conscience, empathy and all human traits of compassion once held as a priority in society were of no importance while maintaining a viable population to rejuvenate a new world.

Maintaining an existing population and developing new generations to continue meant having limitations. Screening during the medical development of a human eliminated physical deformities and mental inadequacies. At this time, limitations of food, space and care forced these limitations before a human was suitable. When the earth became inhabitable and able to support humans, then compassion would return, and each new life would be cared for and given a chance to assist human advancement.

Tolerance was a luxury that the ocean habitants could not afford to consider with leniency. A corrupt mind, an evil mind, a destructive mind had to be eliminated. Criminals at all stages of development were eliminated. Unfortunately, a criminal mind can not be screened at conception. A criminal develops as the mind grows. A criminal does not ensure the success of a habitat. Elimination is a must and is dealt with immediately.

These ocean habitats have survived through these thousands of years because of a desire to maintain a human existence in hopes of populating a new earth world. Observations of the humans that remained on the land, confirmed that strict rules of society would maintain a viable human race. Being ocean bound, and in a sense secured by distance and water depth, land dwellers and the criminal aspect were unable to penetrate habitats and inseminate their criminal intent. A valued monetary currency did not exist. A sharing system worked because there was no need to posses for the gratification of greed.

Humanity collapsed among those that remained to occupy the declining land surface. Intense heat; destructive storms, rising flood waters, volcanic eruptions, and deaths from human predators, including animals, reptiles and insects eliminated most of the land-based humans. Diseases; those that naturally inflict humans, and those created by nature and man's own lack of hygiene reduced an extreme portion of humans. Those that were left managed to eliminate themselves.

This world consisted of the haves and have-not. Those of monetary substance were unable to buy their future existence. Money had no value because society did not create a sustaining base. Societies' farmers, ranchers and processors could not grow produce, sustain meat products when the land became sterile. The takers emerged; the criminal minded, and subordinates ruled the world.

A possessive criminal mind desires to take and hoard from those that will not freely give. Eliminating humans that resist is a minor act when want is the agenda. A criminal pyramid exists with a ruling dictator dominating over subordinates. Each individual vying for the coveted top position. The down fall of the pyramid is not internal conflict and elimination. Lack of humans to cultivate and produce substance has brought down the criminal pyramids. When the single thought of acquiring wealth, means eliminating the source producers then the produce dwindles. Implosion occurs when the remaining wealth is internally fought over. Elimination of criminal pyramids is wagged between similar opponents until a single survivor eliminates itself. Over a short period of time, the criminal aspect of humanity on the remaining land was eliminated.

Humans became eradicated during the heating cycle and glacial cycle of the earth, by their own dysfunction. From over-population to threatened, to vulnerable, to extinct, humans were eradicated. Those beings of human composition that survived in obscurity in small pockets regressed to a primitive existence of mentality and culture.

It seemed that the ocean inhabitants had maintained structure; though some aspects of technology declined; scientific advances progressed. There was no indication of success of the space migration. If reaching a hospitable planet, were they able to advance or did they regress to a rebirth state of mankind? From the progression of oceaners to becoming landers, it was a lesson in understanding how early humans progressed. Having retained advanced knowledge and logical thought process, survival on the rebirthing land became a mixture of all time-frames from caveman to nomads; agriculturists, stone age, medieval, industrialist, scientific, electronic and futuristic. Advanced knowledge had to accept and adapt to a world that was rebirthing and only offered the basics of resources.

Beneath the retreating glaciers, beneath the cultivated earth remained substance of the twenty-first century laying above all preceding changes in earth's deaths and rebirths.

SIX

Upon a grassy plateau, the abundance of fauna had lasted through the late summer seasonal quarter. With the bitter winds on the higher elevation, it was no longer suitable to camp in the open. Under a canvas dome huddled around the centre stove, Ed, May and Jill absorbed the heat venting to fill the comfortable dome. Having apprenticed with an elder goat herder, Ed had ventured out on his own. After two seasonal quarters, and at an age of twenty-two seasons, Ed ventured out with a young herd. Standing at five-feet-ten inches tall, his slim frame was suited to the wandering life of a herder. Being a product of the ocean habitat, he was not suited for the confines of a structure surrounded by water. The vastness of the landscape appealed to senses.

May had met Ed when both landed at a land departure compound. Whether it was an instant attraction or the fact that May overheard information that Ed was destined to travel the landscape as a shepherd, she decided to approach with a cohabitation contract. Delicate in appearance, yet robust with an average build at five-feet-five inches, May argued her case to bashful Ed. Educated in Geology, she wanted to scour the landscape to study earth's changes.

From a distance, May watched a young man loading a portable land crawler with supplies. The land crawler is basically a six-foot wide by ten-foot long box on two tracks. Above the five-foot walls, solar panes energized the storage batteries below the box and between tracks. External levers, controlled direction of the slow-moving crawler. The young man hobbled four mature goats then checked a supply list; dome tent, animal care products, stove, dry food supplies, clothes, basic dome furnishings consisting of bed and furniture. The lifting front wall of the crawler would accommodate room to ride under during inclement weather.

May's mind calculated the remaining space in the crawler's box, 'Enough room for my gear, and for Jill's.'

"What are you thinking?" Jill asked, disturbing May's thoughts. "I thought we were going to travel together?"

"We are, with a slight alteration." May's smile brightened the brown freckles on pronounced cheeks.

May and Jill were a rare birth from a single birthing host. Though of different eggs and sperm; May's complexion of grey-white was highlighted by brown freckles and long white hair. Jill contrasted with long black hair, brown complexion and greyish shade patches. At the same height as May, Jill filled out her frame. By an odd necessity, the two remained close during rearing. The sharing of a womb bonded the females despite the cold clinical structure of the ocean habitat's mandate.

Jill also differed in education, selecting to study Meteorology. Though Meteorology and Geology differed, both had affected the earth's changes. May and Jill decided to venture across the landscape and study their diverse fields together.

"Why not travel with that young fella. Plenty of room in his land crawler," May pointed out the shepherd fussing with care over the goats. "A shepherd is stable, caring, and kind of suitable for cohabitation. Shepherds are slow travellers, so by tagging along, it will give us plenty of time for us to do field study. We won't have to worry about our own crawler, and I bet he can cook?"

A smirk twisted Jill's lower lip as sneering eyes inspected the crawler assigned to them. Upon viewing the crawler, she instantly resented the idea of driving, maintaining and having to divert time away from scientific study. "I hate cooking as much as the site of this contraption." Turned away from May, Jill stared down trying to intimidate the mechanical beast. "I fear that you have a plan?" she said to empty space where May had been standing.

May did not intend to approach the shepherd empty handed. A round scroll document was gripped confidently in a hand. The mindset of humanity had changed since the corrupted ages of the twenty-first century. No longer was sex a taboo, nor a male dominated society. With a specified breading program to maintain a continuous population, the free female governed their bodies, functions and pleasures. Taking the structure of bee and ant cultures, humans derived a sterilization program for female and male populations that would be designated as the labour population. Only special females would be selected as breeding hosts. Human embryos and sperm would be harvested from adolescents at the age of puberty before their sterilisation program.

Cohabitation was a contract agreement controlled by the female for duration and selected male. Male mentality welcomed the ease of selection, and if able to provide the stability of cohabitation and perform with sexual satisfaction, a contract could last indefinitely. Though May had derived an alternative reason to approach the shepherd with a cohabitation contract, she did possess instant affection for the male.

"Excuse me," May boldly said, bending towards the man tending to the goats. "May I inquire?"

A curious goat licked at May's long white hair. Turning head and eyes from the hobbles on a goat's front legs to works boats, Ed's curiosity climbed legs and torso to meet warm brown eyes of a female. A flush of heat tinted his slate grey facial skin. A shyness within Ed's makeup proved that he was suited to animal communication. He stuttered a hello.

"Yes . . ., Miss."

"May . . ., and you are?"

The woman's voice sounded sweet and soft, a sound reminiscent of a purring baby goat. "Ah . . ., I'm . . ., I'm a shepherd . . .,"

"Yes, I assumed, but your name?"

Ed watched May's empty hand caress a goat's warm snout. "Me, my name . . ., is . . ., Ed . . ., I'm a shepherd."

May's warm understanding smile was not condescending towards Ed's awkwardness. Jill watched the unfolding act of negotiations, seduction, manipulations and a forthcoming agreement or possible breakdown. Finding May's boldness somewhat deceiving, Jill rooted for May's deception. Maybe Jill was selfish, for she did not relish the thought of cooking, or maintaining the crawler, not to mention setting up camp, taking down camp and cooking! After-all, the shepherd would have to do his own camp set-up, cook and handle the crawler; so why not lend him a hand.

From a distance, Jill could not hear a conversation even when leaning forward with a hand cupped behind an ear. Gestures and body mannerisms were visible, and Jill understood their context. May was obviously in control, offering positive suggestions. Ed's lips barely responded, though positive confirmation by a nodding head was in May and Jill's favour. A climax of negotiations was about to happen. Jill saw May unroll the cohabitation contract and present it to the shepherd. The moment of truth; no, the man was shaking his head no, it swayed from side to side then hands patted his chest then he lifted a hand in an uncertain gesture.

Intense hope drained from Jill's stance. Heavy disappointment slumped her body onto flat feet and limp arms drained warmth. All was over. Jill's wide green eyes followed the man turning away from May left holding an extended scroll. He reached into a pack then turned back to the contract. An object in his hand hovered over the cohabitation contract.

"Whew . . .," Jill's exhaled breath exclaimed. "I wonder what May said to convince him? I don't have to cook!" Excited feet stomped a dance of victory into the dust.

Though smitten by the bold female, Ed felt that the responsibility of caring for a female was a burden. Similar with the mentality of sheep and goats, which are followers and need to be led, Ed was also a follower. Caring for a flock and leading a herd was Ed's ability, though he also liked to be cared for and led. Having someone making decisions about every other aspect of life, other than his herd seemed logical. While a flushing red altered his weathered brown face, Ed signed the cohabitation contract.

Anxious to be on his way to an assigned apprenticeship, Ed stood bashfully at the front of the crawler. He and four curious goats watched the excited females transfer their gear and scientific equipment into the crawler. Feeling that he should help, a shyness and the fact that May stated that they would do their share, held him back. Anyway, the other female scared him. Upon introductions, she boldly stated, 'I do not do the cooking'. Ed wondered what else she did not do?

When the back door was closed, Ed engaged the forward gear on the crawler. Taking a bearing westward to the grass plains, he began to herd the anxious goats towards munchable foliage. At a slow pace, the crawler moved barely faster than a human walking speed. With a suitable speed, the goats had a leisurely access for feeding and wandering. Ed guided the goats while being aware of predators, the crawler's heading and the wandering locations of his new travelling companions. Just as eager as Ed was to his trade, May and Jill wandered freely to apply their trades.

Though eyes were cautious of predators, Ed felt secure when a hand touched the pistol on a hip belt. Understanding the devastation of humanity and earth-bound creatures, the world's surviving societies eliminated the mentality of eradicating wildlife. Harvesting from a sustainable creature for food was controlled. Eliminating predators because of fear, or dislike was abolished. Weaponry carried by landers housed tranquilizers to suspend creatures until humans could escape. Predators were allotted the chance to survive based on nature's ability to sustain both herbivores and carnivores.

Selecting a distant location, Ed calculated the crawler's speed and the limited light at day's end to stop and set up camp. Allowing the goats to eat, Ed still managed to keep them heading in a comfortable pace towards the advancing crawler. Intent on applying their knowledge gained, May and Jill plied their independent trades. With a cautious eye, Ed scanned for indications of wildlife, especially predators.

On the landscape carved relatively flat by advancing glaciers, it did leave remnants of debris in its receding wake. Every rock, stone, pebble was of interest to May; mineral content, dispersion, and for pleasure the simple beauty of colours along with the smoky to clarity of quarts.

Unknown to Ed, Jill's ability to test the weather would have benefits when feeding, travelling and seeking cover based on weather patterns and forecasts. At this early state of applying his trade, Ed was unable to read the weather, or to plan a day based on forthcoming weather. Ed's current plan was based on a time schedule; up at dawn, pack gear into the crawler, water stock, travel in four hour increments then unpack gear and set up camp for the night. He did not figure on the weather interrupting a schedule.

Adjusting and testing equipment, Jill focused on current conditions, a means of understanding the weather over a vast landscape. Having knowledge of ocean weather conditions from an ocean habitat perspective, this baron landscape was foreign and challenged her perspective of unknow weather conditions. Eyeing three-hundred and sixty degrees of perspective of land, horizon and sky, she proclaimed the day calm with no threats.

May doted at every surface rock, observed some, neglected others, and some were retrieved and placed in a pack. Ed walked in pace with the small herd of four goats; walked as if they were leading rather than a staff urging the four-legged creatures forward. Turning eastward to view their path, Jill's reflective eyes stared at her elongating shadow. Knowing of shadow effects, this effect when alone on a vast empty landscape has a spirited consequence. Though alone, she was not alone, her essence of existence was reflected upon the ground; to accompany and be a reassuring friend.

In the unknown lapse of time, Jill realized the meaning of the elongated silhouette. Turning quickly westward, eyes picked out the crawler stationary and Ed making camp. May was making her way across the red haze of a setting sun. Dust particles lifted from the baron lands will tint the sky reddish until the earth is able to green itself with vegetation. Gathering equipment, she headed towards the crawler. A flash of darkness, a speck crossing her peripheral view was of little concern to conscious thought.

Noticing Jill approaching, May waited and together they entered the camp site Ed had set up. By the crawler, the goats lay tethered for the night. Two dome abodes stood between the goats and the open-faced cook stoves. A sweet aroma of stew simmering reached the nostrils of the females.

"May," Jill whispered, a tone of grieving joy. "He has cooked. Has he cooked for all of us?"

"Yup, his suggestion." May's smile a reflection of making a good deal on the cohabitation contract, though wondering if a six-month duration was sufficient. The cohabitant's first night would reveal more insight for Ed and May.

"I don't have to cook, just eat?" Jill rejoiced in silence while eyes took in details. "Ed has put up two waste elimination units."

May was somewhat puzzled, wondering if Ed was being hesitant to sharing, or maybe was concerned about their modesty in mixed company. Was he being shy, reluctant to commence cohabitation right off the bat on their first night?

"He did cook for all of us, didn't he?" hope drained from Jill's elated face. "Two waste units, two domes, two cook stove units. He is sitting in a chair on one side, and our chairs are together on this side. He only cooked for himself. I bet your stuff and mine are in the same dome unit."

"I'll take care of matters," May's voice crumbled with determination. Placing her gear in the crawler, tired feet and legs stomped towards the cookstove. The aroma of food confused her emotions.

Removing a battered hat, Ed stood respectfully to greet travelling companions. An awkward timid smile broadened as wide eyes focused on May's stern facial features.

"Hello Ladies. The meal is ready. Would you prefer bowls or plates for the stew? There is pan bread in a dough oven on the second stove. I figured that by using two stoves; well more room, I baked a pie too. This was a long first day, so a good meal is deserving. I figured using both waste elimination units; in that way both can be used at the same time, no need for anyone to wait. Both stocked; shower ready, warm water and towels waiting. I supplied my stock. Not right for me to rumble through a woman's gear. Meal ready when you are ready."

Abruptly becoming silent, and turning to fidget at the stew, Ed placed the hat on. Confused, May and Jill shrugged. With determined anger defused, May took Jill's arm and headed to the domes.

"I think Ed has used up his dialogue quota. I couldn't get a word out of him before. And, everything he said makes sense," whispered May, suddenly hesitant when standing before the domes.

"I don't have to cook . . ., ever?" Jill danced on the spot, eager to enter a dome, then hesitated.

"His boots are in front of that one." Suddenly, May's previous anger rose. "I wonder if my gear is in his dome?"

Rushing into the dome, Jill quickly stuck a frowning face back out. "Nope, all in here."

"Well, that is going to change," a grumble forced it way out between clenched teeth.

Forcing her way past Jill, May's long white hair trailed her annoyance. In minutes, all of her gear was transferred into Ed's habitat dome. May settled in with no fuss. Emerging after a shower and ready for an evening meal, May joined Jill in approaching the cook stoves emitting warmth.

"Ed will be surprised when retiring," said Jill leaning girlishly against May.

"He'll get over it." May's smile beamed warm and her voice lost the remnants of earlier anger.

From a distance a low grumble vibrated through on air and through the peaceful camp.

SEVEN

Through the evening the newly arranged travellers became acquainted from awkward moments of life's details to the laughter of becoming friends. Suddenly a silence engulfed the campground and voices became mute. The lateness had exhausted suitable conversation topics, and bodies craved sleep. Only popping sounds of the burning fuel in the stoves echoed in the cooling night of the spring quarter. Ed deliberately prolonged the hours with questions to keep the females talking. An ear was always cautious of a grumbling sound just beyond the limit of camp-light reflection.

"Ed, sure can't take a hint," Jill whispered, her dark hair swaying side to side with admonishing disappointment. "You should have taken the cave-woman tactic and dragged him by the ear to the dome shelter."

"He'll show up . . ., eventually," quipped May, her thoughts settled on the fact that a first night of companionship would be awkward anyway. Besides, sleep was more important to rejuvenate the tiring day. "Where-else is he going to sleep . . ., with the goats?"

Jill's mocking, nodding head went unnoticed as May entered the dome. Dropping clothes and side arm to the floor as if shedding skin, sleep brought her into deep repose when snug under the bed coverings.

Knowing that an unidentified prowler had been lurking in the edge of darkness, Ed remained stationary waiting for a visual. Dousing the cookstoves and diming the camp site lights, he resumed watch. A thumb unlatched the holster strap then cocked the pistol's hammer head into a safety position. Cartridges held moderate charges to disable most predators for thirty minutes without lasting complications. Once a predator was identified then a safe dosage would be injected to allow suitable time for humans to travel to a safe destination.

Knowing that inquisitive eyes were watching, Ed slowly made a campsite inspection, checking the crawler and domes for any visible prints. Lastly, he checked the goats. They were resting, though heads and eyes were alert, sensing another creature in the vicinity. Satisfied that all was calm, Ed's light steps backed into the dim edge of the darkness. Looking inward into the campsite allowed better viability than blindly gazing into the darkness. The unknown predator would be more interested in potential within the camp than an object leaving.

Besides being a shepherd, Ed had studied wildlife biology, an interest associated to the care of domesticated stock. Being an oceaner only allowed for aquatic species. Now that he was a lander, each new encounter with any species of land animal would be exciting and of valued scientific study. This first experience was also training in action, a means of understanding animal characteristics pertaining to specific animal traits. Ed still did not know what the predator was.

When successful in tranquilizing the animal, he would measure; inspect condition, observe physical structure, then become acquainted with prints, previous vocal sounds, and their patterns of tracking and stocking. Fear of the unknown was present, though curiosity overrode the potential of damage that a predator could inflict on humans and livestock. Ed should have been aware of this and prevented himself from believing that no harm would come to himself, companions and stock. At this moment, he trusted ability to hit a target with a first shot, and that the injection would be active.

Shivers tingled hairs on the back of his neck sending a cool then warm flush through his body. A sudden awareness of vulnerability urged head and eyes to quickly turn about to face an approaching predator. Forcing a ridged body to remain in position, eyes darted to a shadow just beyond the stoves. A black form entered the dim light, large paws preceding a lowered head and large torso and shoulder hump.

'A bear,' Ed said in thought, proud of his ability to identify. 'Highly dangerous, both claws and teeth can instantly kill. Ideal location for injection is the front portion of the shoulder hump just ahead of the front quarter.'

Withdrawing the firearm, Ed leveled an aim and waited for the full advancement of the beast. A close shot would be best, fired at the climax of its approach, a moment before it pounces on an intended prey. The bear knew where the goats were and the hiding place of the humans. Pouncing on prey would be in good time for the bear is also a curious creature, wanting to inspect this strange apparition popping up in the emptiness of the landscape.

'Wait, wait.' Ed's finger against the pistol's trigger felt cramped, as hands steadied the L-shaped firearm. 'It will pause at the chair under the dim light, it is going to sniff where I sat . . ., now!'

Goat heads turned towards the swoosh sound of the firearm ignition, then to the thud sound of the dart head hitting its mark against the bear's hump. Small beady eyes on a twisting head inspected the impact area. Both the slight thud, pick and swoosh sound was odd and curious until instant sleep toppled the bear to the ground. As if undisturbed, the campsite continued its slumber.

Only for a moment did Ed allow pride to assume the spotlight. He now had to take statistics, decide on a suitable dosage and drag the bear from the campsite. Approaching the slumped creature, it was much smaller than first visualized. Ed determined it to be of a full season and a half old. Just a young curious juvenile, though still potentially dangerous.

Satisfied that all information was documented, Ed began the task of dragging the brown bear to a safe distance. The approximate two-hundred pounds was laborious to drag, yet not difficult. Calculating the remaining hours of darkness and the time required to pack up camp and travel a safe distance, Ed fixed portions of tranquilizing liquid.

As the light of morning tinted the sky on the horizon, Ed had packed most of the camp into the crawler. A breakfast on the move had been prepared for companions. Bewildered by the quick morning departure, May and Jill stared at Ed's happy morning face.

"I will explain after we are on the move. I need to show you an amazing creature."

Ed's smiling face could not be argued with, whether May and Jill wanted to, after all, they had attached themselves to his crawler.

"Did Ed sleep with the goats last night?" Jill personally asked, her warm breath against May's ear.

"I think so. There is a strange smell floating about him." May offered a whimsical smile towards Ed as he entered the dome.

As the crawler began its forward travel, three bodies hovered around the sleeping bear. Pesky flies basked in the bear's body heat rising from silky brown fur.

"That was in our camp last night?"

"Sure was, Jill," Ed said somewhat boastful.

"And we were in danger?"

"No . . ., could have been. No . . ., my shot was accurate."

May adjusted the holster on a waist belt. "I didn't think . . ., on our first night as landers . . ., I've never practised shooting."

"I will make sure everyone is up to standards." Bending, Ed brushed flies from the bear's moist eyes. "I put a paste over the eyes to protect them from flies and the sun. It will wake in about an hour and will be confused. It will stay in place until able to rub the paste from eyes. I've left some dried fruit to keep it occupied. By the time it is on the move, we should be well away."

Leading off, Ed followed the crawler and goats randomly munching short grass. Tagging behind with fear of being followed, May and Jill's heads randomly looked back at the sleeping mound of bear flesh.

Realizing that being a lander exposed them to all that nature provided, May and Jill learned quickly to be aware and become efficient with firearms and timed doses of tranquilizers. Living off the bounty of the land also means adjusting food intake and supplementing with plants. Slowly the stock of medicines provided by the ocean medical dispensary dwindled. Both May and Jill felt a strangeness of body changes and emotions that they could not explain. Unlike the females, Ed had discarded all medications and supplements on the first day of setting foot on land. His thoughts were, 'if one must exist on land, then one must benefit from the land, not products that are only available on the ocean habitat'. What he began to sense was a sexual drive, which May responded to, though he could not understand the varied emotions expressed by May. With suppressed humour he noticed that Jill mimicked May's symptoms.

By the fall season, the trio reached the compound of the goat and sheep herder. Ed began an assigned two-year apprenticeship. Given the duration of time in one place, May and Jill now had a base site to work from. Jill offered a six-month cohabitation contract with the resident herder. Infatuation did not last through the length of the contract. Jill was a bit envious of May's success with Ed. They were so different; Ed being reserved, stable and unexcitable, where May was eager, forthright and expressive. Yet, they were able to meld when together.

In the spring season of Ed's second year and gaining knowledge of animal husbandry and care, it was time to venture forth on his own. Ed, May, Jill and the accumulated tribe of goats headed north to untouched lush grasslands. The spring and summer weather was too good to be true, according to Jill's weather studies and forecasts based on studies she had conducted over the past two-years. A bold prediction was that fall, and winter weather would be vengeful. She suggested that they head south and find a compound to hunker down in for the duration of the long winter.

Listening to a howling wind brushing against the fabric of the dome, Jill and Ed viewed a map created of the area. From observations and existing crude maps, Ed had pieced together a suitable map. Most locations and landmarks were speculative, for Ed had not been to all the locations.

"The most logical place to overwinter would be," Ed pointed to a map site directly south. "A good three-month travel, and that would be pushing it."

Jill's concern eyes inspected May's flush face and prone frame stretched out on a bed. May smiled back as she wiggled swollen toes towards the stove.

"May could ride in the crawler most of the way," Jill suggested, a deep concern for May's health held deep in thoughts.

"I'm a bit bloated, not an invalid." May's freckled cheeks sparkled from the stoves reflective light. "If a pregnant nanny can walk, so can I. I've got plenty of time."

A stern frown etched with condescending anger showed on Jill's patched complexion. "You don't know how far along you are. You are just guessing . . ., at four or is it six months?"

Unlike having a cold, indigestion or even a broken bone where anxiety, depression and discomfort worries both body and mind, this current sensation was accepted. Body changes and emotions was not feared. Surprisingly, May wanted to experience this evolution, even though she had no idea how she was able to become impregnated. What was developing within felt natural, as if human gestation was normal, an everyday occurrence. May wondered why Ocean Habitats had developed a birthing program, and why all females were not allowed to experience conception, gestation and birthing? For whatever reasons, she would experience giving life. Concerns, yes. Worry, expected. Wanting and accepting, a natural procedure that May was emotionally uplifted by, an almost spiritual encounter. Without know why, this was just life unfolding.

Inside Ed's mind thoughts were expressive words of anger, concern and fear. His mouth stayed shut, though warm eyes stared deep into May's creamy brown eyes.

"Just . . ., okay, maybe a bit past four." May caressed a slight belly bump. "Ed, . . ., tell Miss worry-wart that a goat can go five months before really showing, and still walk a good day's distance."

A demand. May gave Ed a demand, and based on May's emotional swings, he had to give an answer. "I never push pregnant goats, and usually it is half the normal speed. Most of the females are pregnant, but they are not due until the spring quarter."

"That's not an answer," May voiced, scolding Ed.

'I should have kept my mouth shut,' Ed's inner voice said. 'What do they call it, hormone alteration?' Adverted eyes turned to the map. "There are other compounds scattered about, and some may have suitable accommodations and feed. Some may be abandoned."

"Which ones might?" asked Jill, also wanting to avoid a verbal battle with May.

Staring over a rising belly, May inspected plump toes. "Are my feet swelling?" she asked to no-one in particular yet expecting a reply.

"Nope," Ed quickly replied. "The shadow of diffused light makes everything look plump." Turning to face May, he puffed up cheeks in a subliminal action.

"Show me where the compounds are?" asked Jill, directing dialogue away from May's intent topics.

Dragging a finger across the rough surface of the goat-hide map, eyes picked out locations marked by an x with a circle. An x within a circle indicated fixed compounds. An x alone was just a location of a possible camp site or a land mark. A circle alone meant a compound with no livestock or feed.

"I'm not sure of exact locations, they are just dots on the map. All, except one are beyond a three-month reach. It is a trip directly south or directly west to a compound on the plain."

Dragging a finger back and forth between their location on the plateau and the circled x on the plain, Ed thought of complications that would be encountered in either direction. "South is warmer and grasslands. West is shelter, feed and humans."

"Humans that may know more about May's situation."

"What situation, Jill?" May said in a tone that hinted at aggravation. "Nannies drop kids all the time without problems. How hard can it be?"

"Have you ever seen a human baby born, cared for one? I haven't. The ocean habitat birthing unit took care of all babies until ready for schooling." Jill's face tensed as a final burst of words forced through pressed lips, "You're not a goat."

Fear gripped Ed's throat as a chill rushed over accumulating goosebumps. "We are heading west to the compound, no arguments. Be ready at dawn.

EIGHT

Knowing that repopulating the earth with inhabitants, the ocean birthing program was dedicated to producing humans that would be durable and sound. Controlled creation provided units that would be suitable. Early detection eliminated the unwanted, the defective. Emotion was not a factor in deciding the continuation or elimination of a fetus. A population was needed to inhabit the earth and allowed to prosper. Survival superseded the ability and emotional aspects of sustaining and caring for hindered human beings.

Survival of the fittest was a reality of all creatures and was proven over the recorded twenty-first century history. The criminals, takers, leachers, dependants, and hoarders of monetary currency all perished because each could not use basic skills of survival to sustain one's self by cultivating and harvesting substance. Farmers, harvesters and gathers would survive. Criminals tried to intimidate, take, covet, and eliminate subordinates and hierarchy until reaching prominence for themselves. They eliminated each other along with leachers, weak dependents and hoarders. Drug users, producers and sellers had eliminated themselves early during the collapse of society. Currency had lost value. One could not buy sustenance. Wealth and power was self-eliminating.

Survival is selfish and with the destruction of an economy and social structure, each human able to sustain life discarded the weak, old, sick, mentally challenged and the disabled. All human emotion of respect, devotion, empathy was discarded for the need of self preservation. A simple mentality based on sustenance prevailed over brawn and greed. When society gains social stability will compassion towards those of challenges be extended.

For these reasons, ocean habitats had collectively developed a breading program to produce a single human population containing a mixture of all previous races. No longer existed individualized humans. All colours, tones, features, mannerisms and languages became singular, a mixture of all in each human. DNA of an individual became an equal percentage of all previous human races. Gone was race prejudices. Each human was linked genetically to each other. Thousands of years during the decline of the earth and the rebirthing of the earth surface allowed for the birth of a single mixed race of humans.

Sterilization of juvenile adolescents of male and female would prevent the continuation of a single race developing. All inhabitants of the ocean habitats accepted the procedure, allowing the birthing department to create humans of mixed contributions of eggs and sperm. Within generations a singular race of humans did not exist. Yet the sterilization of adolescents approaching puberty continued.

Youth venturing onto the rebirthing earth did not dwell on the though of reproduction of humans among themselves. Society was ingrained to accept the established ocean birthing program. Mutual sex acts became an open expression to be shared without complications.

May and Jill had not considered possibilities of their bodies reproducing. Nor did they have knowledge of how their own bodies worked, or if being able to reproduce. Ed's familiarity of animal husbandry was knowledge of the functionality of reproduction. Yet he accepted the fact that all males at puberty, after a medical procedure to have sperm harvested, then became sterile. Unconsciously, the trio discontinued all medications when becoming landers. Had nature assumed the control of reverting the sterilization of humans? Had evolution manifested a need for humans to reproduce on the rebirthing earth? Had a random chance connected Ed and May, resulting in a impregnation of sperm and egg?

Medications were prescribed to be consumed as a bulk supplement. Though aware of the list of functions of the medications to counter; malaria, measles, mumps, hepatitis, cancers and the multiple of the twenty-first century diseases, each person individually decided to stop. As landers, each accepted the fact that their survival would be a process of combative action when encountering problems. Reversal of sterilization was not considered. Now that reproduction was engaged, wonderment, bewilderment and fear entered thoughts.

May's mood swings, morning retching and bloating could not be explained. Ed's visual comparison of May's extended stomach to that of a pregnant goat suggested the possibility of human pregnancy. Ignorance is bliss when complications are not considered. May expressed joy when a baby goat was born and expected a similar ease of human birth, followed by emotional wonderment. Ed saw the pain of labour that the female goat endured and the indifferent attitude of the buck. Only Ed witnessed a still birth and the personal emotion experienced when discarding the limp form.

Reaching the compound on the Northern plain was Ed's determination. Maybe a lander would have knowledge and provide assistance. Rarely had he assisted in the birth of a goat kid. On rare occasions, he had to assist by pulling on legs to extract a kid. Would he have to tug on a human baby and break the birthing sack then stick a finger into the mouth to clear mucus? Would it be as simple as that? Would the first 'bahh' be heard? Ed did not know what sound a human baby would make.

The act of sexual activity had been taken for granted, with no after-the-act repercussions. What had twenty-first century ancestors done; refrained from multiple encounters, or only engage for the purpose of reproductions, or welcomed births every nine months? Ed recalled the gestation times of goats at six months, bovine at nine months, chickens at twenty-eight days, humans at nine months. A snickered though of fearful humour was repelled by the thought of a human being born in twenty-eight days. This new rebirthing earth would be repopulated in a matter of months.

Shacking the thought out of his mind, Ed exited the dome to greet the assault of pelting ice crystals.

NINE

A blast of wind carried the first hint of the coming winter seasonal quarter as it dropped off the edge of the receding glacier face. Cold wind gathered speed after dropping onto the plain and gathered up dry soil to mix with ice crystals. With no natural formations to alter its attack, the wind headed towards the compound. Snug within the domes, Mat, Kat and livestock did not anticipate the advancing storm. Sleep was undisturbed as wind, sand and snow pellets swirled around and past the dome's shelters.

Built squat against the earth, the dome design weathered well against all that nature hurled with intent to destroy. Even the calm and seemingly passive delivery of heat and scorching rays of sunlight was deflected from the dome's interior. Simple ingredients of sand, clay, lime, water and weaved members, when combined formed a concrete substance of suitable stability. A glazing compound of silica was baked onto the outer surface as a waterproof and wind-proof barrier. Built to a thickness of twelve inches allowed for coolness within during heated seasons and able to retain heat during cold seasons. Having limited exterior openings, conditions of weather were not observed until exiting.

Acting upon an ingrained action repeated over the season, each day when waking, Mat wobbled to the exit door. What the day promised would be observed when opening the door to view what was presented. Today the pressure of the moving storm sucked the door open, ripping it free of Mat's hand grip. Warm interior air was sucked out past Mat's form, rippling clothing. A moving wall of dust and snow prevented ability to view the barn dome across the centre of the compound. At the point where warmth of the interior dropped a degree, he pulled the door closed. Clothing relaxed and agitated hair rested upon his head.

"Not a nice day," Mat said, as if Kat would hear, and the stock across the way would acknowledge. "Is this a day storm or one that will linger for a week or more," again said in general. A small non-descriptive cat cowering behind a clay container listened, though would not respond.

Lingering in position longer than normal, for usually he would step outside to cast a glance about the compound. A debate unfolded in Mat's mind. Priority would be to cross the compound to check the stock, then attend to the methane burner and steam generator. Solar energy would be off-line through the duration of the storm. A forgotten detail fought for consideration while Mat considered having scrambled eggs or poached.

Mat had planed on raising the beacon days earlier but procrastinated during the fine weather. Determining that Tell was only at a day or so distance, there was not a hurry to raise the beacon. Instantly finding that a storm was upon the compound and visibility limited, Tell would need the beacon for a visual destination point.

"Scrambled eggs, then check stock and generator, then the beacon." A head of matted hair nodded and an eye caught view of the small cat. "I suppose that you could care less, but if I mention breakfast, you will be at my heels?"

Cat ears twitched, and eyes widened with forlorn innocence.

Bundled in a goat hide coat, Mat eagerly met the first storm of the winter season head on. Land temperature had not yet cooled and conflicted with the biting edge of the wind. Fresh snow was not falling; the snow crystals were layers swept off the glacier. Added dust from the plains created a haze that prevented long-distance visibility.

Tell would need a line of sight and an object to focus on. Having no guidance other than visual landmarks, missing a destination by feet is definitely probable. He wondered why Mat had not raised the beacon? Though being a week early, Tell was confident that Mat would have the light up. Could something be wrong? Worry lines creased Tell's forehead turning wrinkles white against weathered skin.

Leaning against the wind, Mat dragged out the tethering cable for the beacon. 'I should have done this two weeks ago, instead of playing in that cave.' Thoughts focused on the possible trove within the cave while his body tackled the physical aspect of the current task.

A mountain of earth had been pushed by the advancing glacier against ancient twenty-first century buildings. A reactive force of some sort prevented the earth and glacier from crumbling and destroying a central structure. The structure must have been a federal building of some sort; maybe an archive suppository, a library or a museum? Besides the cook book brought home for Kat, Mat had viewed a significant find. Through an opening, he shone a light on a train car, or trolley car from the past. Lettering above window openings had to be guessed due to the layers of dust and debris. 'Cana-i-n Pa-cific R-, was all that was legible. Based on the knowledge of longitude and latitude of the world and the potential distance of the advancing glacier, Mat assumed that the words were Canadian Pacific Railway. Noting that the artifact was in a building, he concluded that part of the crushed building had indeed been a museum.

Having stretched out the one-hundred-foot cable, Mat turned to view a wall of invisibility. The compound and domes had vanished from sight. Belief remained that the compound existed. Tracing the cable to its source brought him back to the maintenance dome. Fear of being lost irritated the back of his mind. Unspoken thoughts demanded that Kat stay put inside, and that the livestock had survival instinct to remain in the barn dome. Shadows of Bud, the donkey, and Wojo, the hound could faintly be seen in the barn opening. Mat had faith in the pair. If by chance, they noticed Mat missing longer than necessary, the pair would begin to search. Wojo using scent ability and Bud being the muscle to provide transportation. Both companions were in advanced years, and mat did not want to strain their resources. In the minds of the pair, duty superseded limited strength and declining youth. Allegiance between man and animal is a bond that cannot be explained, though has existed since all creatures have inhabited this earth.

Trudging past the duo; Mat noticed their eyes following, and a hidden thought in their minds, 'Why don't you come in where it is warm?' As if understanding, dog and donkey language, Mat's thoughts responded. 'I'll be in after I get this beacon up.'

Fixing the electric line to the methane generator, a flicked switch illuminated the globe at the end of the cable. Bud and Wojo turned towards the faint glow. Attaching a hose to the holding tank of treated gas from a manure-based fermentation chamber, he rushed to the far end of the cable. Quickly sparking a flint to the ignition, the burner burst into a heat flame. Closing the housing to protect the flame from the wind, it began to inflate a balloon. Expanding with buoyancy, the balloon began to rise, lifting the beacon and cable.

Through the prism configuration of the globe, the light would refract over a great distance and be enhanced by the flame glow within the balloon. High above the ground wind of the mixed snow and dust, the balloon rose to be a guiding beacon for arriving travellers. Though Tell was a seasoned traveller, the beacon would be a welcome gesture. As for the professors, Mat knew that without the beacon, they would aimlessly travel without concern. Not that they were absent minded about priorities; they often became too immersed in debate amongst themselves to bother with daily routines.

Mat laughed to himself upon thinking of the professors. One year the three professors had bypassed the compound four times; each time by a day and within an eight of a mile. They had been debating the existence of a supreme being behind creation of all that exists verses evolution of a single cell over time by adaptation. Eventually by luck, Mat boarded their crawler and stopped it before it ran into the manure stock pile.

Glancing up along the taunt cable, Mat's eyes brightened with pleasure when the sparkling light warmed the dim morning light.

"There it is. Mat would never let me down," Tell bragged, extending hands and arms out front with praise and appreciation. "Sally, is it not a beautiful sight? A warm glow of welcome above the cold harsh storm."

Not being so easily impressed by frills, Sally did experience a warmth by the appearance of the object emerging from the landscape of blandness, emptiness and brutality of weather. "Yeah, somewhat sparkly," she said in a monotone, unexpressive voice. After-all, she did not want to give Tell the impression that she was soft or too emotional. Sally prided herself with being a tough vet, independent and self supporting. She did not want to give Tell the impression of needing the support of a man. Mind you, sex with Tell was good, but this was just a side bonus of cohabitation. Priority was the care of the pregnant bovine.

"It is even brighter in the darkness of night. Many times, it has guided me to the comfort of Mat and Kat's compound. As bright as the brightest of stars and seen from great distances." Settling into the drive seat, Tell became lost in nostalgic thoughts.

"The bovine will be glad to be out of this crawler and able to relax before giving birth. How far away are we?" Sally's eyes drifted away from the mesmerizing light.

"By mid day tomorrow. We will have to stop tonight to reserve power." Tell's excitement energized lazy muscles and he bounced out of the chair. "I'm hungry!"

Cold winds crossed the plateau, carrying remnants of the advancing storm barrelling across the plains. Reaching the edge of the plateau, May disengaged the drive lever of the crawler. Riding in the front compartment, she and Jill were somewhat sheltered from the wind. From their position they peered out in the direction of the plain where the plain should have been.

"I think . . ., I do not want to descend blindly into a soup of unknown depth." May's wide eyes tried to determine where the plateau's decline route began. "If we are not in the right place . . .,"

"We topple over the edge and die. Plain and simple, we camp here for the night." Jill did not mince words of meanings.

Jill's suggestion, no, her demand was all May required to switch the crawler into sleep mode. Fighting against the awkwardness of carrying a frontal bundle, May began unloading gear for a night campsite. Within hours full darkness would be accompanied by bitter cold.

Fighting a frontal wind, Ed struggled to keep the herd of goats moving. Shep, a herd dog continuously nosed laggers to refrain from laying down. Seeing the crawler motionless, he was relieved. Without encouragement, the goats huddled beneath the crawler. Legs curled, and heads nuzzled into a companion's body. Even Shep burrowed into the edge of the huddle. Out of the wind and somewhat content, the goats commenced chewing their cud.

Without words, without the need of suggestions, the three companions set up camp to a basic necessity; a single dome and a single lavatory. Snug in the dome, the stove quickly warmed the area and heated the evening meal. May and Ed watched Jill as she mused over notes and weather charts.

"Based on notes over the past years, there should be no storms this early." Brushing hands through tangled hair, frustration formed altered expressions on her face. "There is a weather cycle that is predictable each year, when or when not, it takes place is random."

Ed wiggled bare toes towards the stove as he readied to put socks and hide boots on. "Your best guess, do we wait until the storm passes or take a chance and push through?"

Placing a coat on, Jill gathered pressure instruments. "My guess is that this is going to be a long storm. If we wait it out, we lose travel time."

Heads turned to observe May. Following the other's lead, she began pulling on clothing. "What . . ., I'm fine . . ., this human is not going to pop out now or in a week. We have plenty of time."

Jill and Ed swayed their heads mockingly.

"I'll take pressure readings and observe the storm's path," said Jill, heading for the door. "Maybe I can sight some landmarks and take a bearing to follow."

Ed rose, straining from the grip of May's hand. A whistle sound echoed as the party exited the dome. High on the plateau the visibility was clear, though a cold wind attacked from the glacier. Eyes glanced out over the plain to see an ocean of swirling dust and snow. Above a dark night sky clearly displaying stars of the universe. A finger pointed, and eyes followed May's indication to an illumination floating above the storm.

"What a beautiful star," May praised the sparkling object.

"It is not natural," Ed exclaimed. "It is human made."

"If humans made it, then they must live there." Hope filled Jill's thoughts when glancing to see May pressing a hand to a rumbling stomach.

"It has to be the compound I told you about, a good month's travelling."

"So, we do not wait out the storm, do we Ed?" Jill nodded, expressing a demand rather than a question.

"We follow the compound star. It sparkles like a star, and we should be able to see it clearly each night."

From the far south, the professors mutually stared out through the crawler's front window. A rolling wall of an approaching storm rolled southward on the plain. Their eyes hovered on the top of the storm and heads swayed from side to side. Professor Art did likewise, though did not know why. The beauty of a destructive force tantalized his artistic side of the brain while a cognitive side asked why the others were transfixed on the storm. Storms had been observed before.

"Professors . . ., what are we observing?"

Pie smirked. "We are not observing, we are searching for the compound light to guide us in."

"Mat always raises a beacon at this time of year."

"A beacon, Story, what does it look like?" Art leaned in parting Phil and Pie.

"You'll know when you see it."

Just at that moment the sparkling reflection of the beacon's prisms cast rays through the top layer of the storm.

"I see it," exclaimed Art. "A magnificent rendition of the Northern Star.

"Star?"

"Sure Pie, Mat's Northern star. Guiding us, as it has each year." Phil sighed and slumped back into the control chair. "If I may have the honour." Phil's hands grasped the crawler's track levers.

"Please do."

"Thank you, Story."

Phil pushed forward on one lever and pulled the opposite. Instantly the crawler jerked as the tracks griped in opposite directions.

"Wrong way Phil. Head toward the beacon," suggested Pie.

Hands altered lever direction. Tracks gouged the soft soil and the crawler altered to a correct heading.

"So sorry, these levers are so confusing." Phil's hands released gripping and shook, shedding the confusion of the operation.

"Phil got us lost once when we let him manipulate these confounded levers."

"Just a day or so," responded Phil to the accusation.

Art peeked at the beacon floating singularly against the dark back ground. "How many travelling days away?"

Pie did a quick calculation before answering, "A couple of weeks, give or take a day or two either way. No more than a month. Just guessing momentarily."

"For a mathematician and engineer, you do a lot of guessing," Art stated.

"I do, don't I!"

Four humans huddled against the cold face of the receding glacier from where the storm originated above. Through the fresh cascade of snow, they could see a faint light piercing randomly through the storm.

TEN

A birthing new world forms danger without notice. The minor of instances will leave ventures' dead or disabled. Descending the glacier after an expedition to study its deterioration, the living and ever-changing landscape swallowed four human males. In a haste to retreat from the glacier surface before winter took advantage, the males left caution slide.

On the vast top of the glacier, the men were indistinguishable from one-another. Warm hides from head to toe shielded their bodies from the biting cold wind. Communication was held silent. If attempting to utter a sound, it would be cast on the wind. Huddled side by side, they trekked southward towards the edge of the glacier. Sleighs tethered behind held their only means of shelter and provisions.

Fears of all sorts played in their minds; the chance of frozen toes and fingers, being frozen in a last step pose, being left behind or separated. A dread of un-spoken events forced the men to group, to feel the pressure of shoulder contact at each step. Obscured faces on moving forms inched forward.

Time and distance were unknown factors. Survival was the ability to step one foot forward and be reassured of shoulder contact. Body movements functioned automatically leaving the mind with task-less duties. Daydreaming functioned as if being reality with visions of reuniting with colleagues at a southern compound; devouring an endless meal, walking on warm sand, or floating on ocean currents, or to the comfort of a crawler left somewhere at the base of the glacier. The whiteness of the surface beneath their feet was invisible to sight.

An ever-changing environment of a revenging ice-age into a rejuvenating inhabitable landscape meant that change must happen. The glacier below their feet would freeze and then thaw, expand and contract. Miles below the thickness of the ice, the warm surface of the earth heated the glacier and began to rot layers from the inside.

In an instant, daydreams vanished to be replaced by an instant review of a life lived in the minds of the men. Weightlessness was only the instant sensation when the surface below their feet gave way. Melting ice turned to water had carved a void within the glacier. A subterranean river flowed towards an exit of unknown origin. Sleighs and shoulder harnesses remained top side as gravity drew bodies into the cavern.

Sensation of free falling limited any ability to react, to even offer verbal or facial reactions. A singular splash would not be heard above the roaring sound of water rushing through a carved-out tunnel. Arms and legs flailed, mouths gasped for air above the water surface. Swept away with the flow of water, bodies were inert objects being flushed out of the interior.

Over multiple years, the water flowed, carving out caverns and river courses. Sallow water depth rushed over smooth ice beds, carrying the men for an unknown distance through the heart of the glacier. In what would have taken a month's travel time on the surface of the glacier, in an hour they were expelled onto the plain in front of the receding glacier. Scrambling onto the land, they huddled to regain warmth. If not for the hides suitable for the environment, the men would likely perish.

Left stranded and without provisions, they will perish. A glimpse of an artificial star above the storm indicated possible habitation. Eyes focussed on the beacon. No words were attempted to be spoken. Each man instinctively knew what must be done. Movement would ward off the chill penetrating their skin. Movement would enhance survival. The star, a beacon of hope would guide them.

One man rose then another, each shaking off excess water and wringing clothing. Following the first man, in single file they headed towards the wall of the storm cascading down from the glacier. Taking a bearing on the beacon, and noting the plateau to the left flank, they walked quickly to build up warmth. Once their body core warmed then they would slow their pace. Without provisions, conserving energy needed to be balanced against time. Reaching the beacon was a gamble, when not knowing the distance. Despite the darkening night, they pushed on.

Nature is unforgiving, and races unbridled. Man, and creatures must accept and learn to adapt. When convenient, avoiding altercations is advised. When necessities arise, combating the elements is to overcome danger to achieve a goal. The men from the glacier needed to survive. Avoiding interaction with the storm would prolong life until deterioration of life. Equally, entering the storm could also end in death. Ed, May and Jill needed to find security of a compound and assistance to sustain life and a new life. When the time indicated morning, despite the lack of light of a storm-free day, Ed edged the crawler down the plateau's incline. Hesitant at fist, Shep began urging the goats to follow.

No-sooner had the crawler angled over the edge and began to rock over rough terrain, is when May experienced the first morning sickness of the day. Helplessly, Jill and Ed watched and listened to May's retching, for neither knew what to do. 'Goats don't heave when pregnant,' Ed had noted, so he had no experience to share. He refrained from saying, 'It will pass.' May's volatile reaction would be unpleasant. Though a female, Jill lacked knowledge, having never been educated on the female reproduction process. The birthing department was off limits to the general population. She and May found it strange being a product of the habitat birthing system, and female, yet be ignorant of the process within the female body. They feared having to experience the unknown and the emotion of birth and possible death of child and mother, because e of lacking knowledge.

Descending from the plateau felt as if the crawler was sinking into a bowl of swirling snow and dust. Soon the light from the beacon would diminish from sight. Only if winds subsided or created vortexes of clarity would the beacon be seen. Shep pressured the goats to follow within touch of the crawler.

Unable to see the landscape ahead, passenger eyes remained fixed forward. Suddenly the crawler nosed into the earth before levelling off. They were on the plain and intent on heading due west toward the beacon. A faint speck flicked then vanished from sight.

"I doubt if we will see the light until night," Ed shouted over the whistle of the wind.

"It feels like we've entered a twenty-four-hour night," said Jill, jotting notes of weather conditions into a log book.

Setting both track levers into an equal speed, Ed locked their positions. He had guessed the last sight location of the beacon and hoped the crawler's direction would be fairly accurate.

As if nature and the earth were angry, this storm raged unabated. A clash of opposing climate weather met over the plains where warm air arrived north at a low altitude, and cold northern hemisphere weather dropped off the receding glacier. Opposing winds clashed and swirled. Sand and dust battled snow and ice crystals for supremacy. Landscape was altered, formations changed, and land creatures suffered. Animals adapted over generations and sought shelter to wait out the weather. Humans also sought shelter, though were often stubborn and tried to defy weather's ability to destroy. Mat and Kat felt secure within the compound domes, and were eager for Tell, and the professors to arrive safely.

Unaware of other travellers in the area, Mat hoped that if there were, the beacon would guide then in. Occasionally travellers had passed through. Only the Doctor was a repeat visitor. With his passing, the professors and Tell became regular seasonal residents. Progression of humans in sustainable numbers was taking a long time to become established landers. A singular birthing program had maintained continuation of humans, though the process was not sufficient enough to increase a land-based population. Where in contrast, wildlife had remained established and multiplied by natural birthing.

May was testing the ability to conceive and deliver a human outside of the established birthing program. The sensation of contraception and feeling body changes of a human developing within wowed May's emotions. Realizing the logic of possible problems were ignored. A joy filled May's thoughts. She was blissfully blessed of not knowing the changes of her body, or what would be experienced during and after child birth. Even Jill and Ed, though more concerned for May's well being, were equally uninformed.

Crowded together on the open front bench of the crawler, eyes searched for glimpses of the beacon. Days had passed with little change in the weather. They had lost contact with the light. Knowing that the crawler's individual track speed was not equal, Ed guessed that their path veered northerly. By what margin of change, he did not know. Caution refused to adjust a direction until spotting the light. Hope of salvation dwindled in the back of their minds.

All possible hope of surviving had vanished from the minds of the four south-bound men. No longer were their minds focused on the future or condition of an existence. Faint glimpses of past-memories sparked within their minds. The ability of the subconscious mind to live within past-memories kept the physical body functioning.

Limp bodies hovered above lumbering legs and feet that plugged aimlessly along. They could no longer remember when the beacon was last seen. The lead man blindly moved forward, his eye sight stricken with snow blindness. Assuming he was searching for recognizable forms, his eyes were unable to distinguish any physical distinctions. Followers focussed on the dark form in front and were led blindly in a wayward direction.

"Bears!" screamed Jill.

Instinctively, Jill drew a cocked pistol and pointed ahead to the blurry objects hoovering in the swirling wind. Four objects seemed larger than normal in the void of white. The dark hide coats were reminiscent of bears, a creature that Jill feared most. Instinct enticed her to pull the trigger rather than question other possible scenarios. She hesitated, undecided as to which bear should receive a tranquilizer first.

"Pull your pistole, Ed," Jill directed, her finger tensing on the cold metal of the trigger. "Shoot the first . . ., I'll shoot . . ., which one Ed . . ., tell me?"

Cowering against Ed's side, May prevented him from disengaging a track lever. Locking the left track, the crawler slowly turned left in an ark. Jill's access for a shot waned as the crawler's wall hid the creatures from sight.

"Why are you turning, they'll come at us from behind." Withdrawing, Jill pressed against a corner of the open cab. "May, draw your pistole."

"I . . ., don't have one."

"Why?" Jill's voice scolded May with a bewildered motherly tone.

"The belt will not fit around my waist . . ., that's why." Hands caressed a protruding belly, indicating the large girth.

"Just hang on a sec until I stop the crawler." Ed locked the right track lever. "In this soupy wind, the objects could be . . ., just land Hoodooos, wind sculptured objects. The mind just assumes what the mind wants them to be. Shep will continuously bark if they are bears."

A single bark sounded as if far away, and barely audible in the constant whistling wind. The companions waited in the open cab, with only Jill holding a pistole in a threatening manner. Always alert, Shep had circled the goats before approaching the strange objects. Expected live animal scent was not detected. A strong pungent aroma of humans at death's door wafted through Shep's nostrils. Cautiously Shep approached the objects and sniffed each one before sitting in front of the lead man.

Fear of the unknown bark instantly froze the men in mid-step. Fight for survival against a predator no longer existed, the men waited for carnivore teeth to pierce through leggings and into wasting flesh. Blind eyes of the lead man searched for an object within the whiteness of his own sight.

Slowly, Ed, then the females cast sight around the edge wall of the crawler to see Shep sitting before statues of black.

"Those are humans," Ed announced rushing towards Shep. "Hello, I'm Ed, a shepherd, and you are?"

73

Heads turned towards the approaching man. Limp bodies gathered around the lead man. Bewildered eyes blinked, as if trying to wipe away the illusion.

"I'm Don. Where are you." Don's eyes circled and rolled.

"Right here," Ed said. A hand raised to sway in front of the man's eyes. "I'd probably say snow blindness. A couple of days of darkness in bandages and you should recover."

A hesitation lingered on both sides until the novelty of meeting other humans in the emptiness subsided. Quick introductions circulated until names became familiar; Jill, Ed, May, Don, Mac, Fred and Sid.

May's intuition about the welfare of the men was instant and before an explanation of the men's state could be explained, she began to bark out orders. Ed and Jill reacted without question. A stove was brought out and ignited to warm the men hunched on the windless side of the crawler. Use to daily setup and take-down, Ed's party had emptied the crawler and had domes set up with heat and food prepared to sustain the men. Ed scoured for suitable blankets while May and Jill tended to the blistering of exposed skin to the cold and abrasive wind. Their greyish skin colour had taken on a sickly green sheen. A compress was placed on Don's eyes and a bandage to prevent eyes from opening. Soon the men were able to rest.

Retired to their own dome after history of events were share between all parties, Ed, Jill and May contemplated this state of affairs. These men needed accommodations and food, while May needed to reach a suitable compound where possible assistance might be during her birthing.

"In a few days, the men will be back to normal and capable to reach a compound south. We need to continue on our path to the nearest compound." Ed's logic was basic, though in his mind he had incorporated multiple details.

Eyes turned to May when she groaned and rolled onto a side. "I think the creature inside me kicked, kicked like a goat." A hand pressed against a side. "We do not know if there is a compound or and humans there to help us?"

"Yes, it is a gamble. If there is no one there, we must move on as fast as possible," Ed added, though failed to provide details, of which the females preferred to hear.

Jill spoke up, knowing that if Ed was not confronted, they would spend the night having to pry each little detail from him. "In one sentence list every detail of your plan. I don't want to spend the night asking questions."

A silence ensued within the dome as exterior wind battered the flesh of the dome. Jill and May stared, their eyes widened with intent to say, 'well answer, Ed'. Ed was thinking, for his eyes were askew upwards.

"Ed . . .?" May whispered softly.

Jill was not as polite, "Well . . .?" she shouted, her voice surely reaching the men in the other dome.

"I'll need more than one sentence."

Flustered, Jill relinquished authority, "Fine, use as many sentences as you want, but, all information in one go."

Taking in a breath of confidence, his chest expanded, eyes widened with courage, as lips mimicked words in silence; practicing before speaking. "We keep only the bare necessities; one dome, one stove, one lavatory unit, sufficient food and clothing. We lighten our load in the crawler; put smaller and weaker goats in the storage area and use maximum speed. Shep will push the rest of the herd to follow. The men will take possession of everything else, including the drag sleigh, and our excess food and several goats. They will be aptly supplied to make their journey south."

"Now, was that so hard to do? Is there anything else you wish to say?" Jill leaned forward daring Ed to say a word.

Thinking eyes rolled searching for a possible subject. Ed's shoulders arched then relaxed as his head swayed no. Jill turned to May, their thoughts seemingly agreeable without need for words.

"Well said, Ed," praised May. "Come to bed. We need to be up and gone by morning."

Ed tuned off the gas light and banked the stove before crawling next to May. Placing a hand on May's stomach, he felt the movement of life settling down. A smile of worry shivered a cold sweat across his brow.

Little had changed in the weather, except for the accumulating amount of snow upon the ground. As was usual, Ed, May and Jill had risen and taken down camp before the visiting men had stirred. Emerging from the dome when hearing the clattering and baying of stirring goats, they faced the accumulation of supplies at the dome entrance. Knowing that Jill would rudely accost him, Ed spurted details is a single go. The men nodded acceptance until the point when Ed mentioned assistance for birthing. Eyes drifted to the goats then hesitantly to May then to her bulging stomach.

"She, you are . . .," Mac began to ask, searching for correct wording.

Jill interrupted the slow thinking men, "It is called being pregnant."

Bemused minds gawked with mixed emotions of wonderment, intertest and childish curiosity. Don's head twitched, his mind searching to see when eyes could not. His hand raised slightly as if wanting to touch, to confirm belief. Mac crouched to stare. Fred's eyes blinked rapidly as if the birthing process would happen instantly. Backing away, Sid feared the unknown. Birthing happened in the confines of the birthing department within habitats, and men were oblivious of suck procedures.

"Landers can't reproduce . . ., landers can have . . .," mumbled Sid, words contradicting words. "How . . ., why . . ., when? Landers are sterile . . ., landers don't. Are you sick? Maybe . . ., there is something . . .?"

"Sid," Don said halting the man's rambling. "Maybe miracles happen. With the rebirth of the land, maybe landers will be able to rebirth the population."

An awkward silence seemed odd surrounded by an angry storm. May felt important, yet resentful of penetrating eyes from the curious.

"We need to go," said Jill, stepping forward to turn May away.

"With snow on the ground, it will be easy to pull the sleigh. Keep the wind at your back and head due south," instructed Ed, a tinge of guilt building for leaving the men to fend for themselves. He was confident on their ability to survive, so selfishness for May's sake eased his conscience.

Leaving the track leavers in their last position before the previous night's diversion, Ed engaged the crawler's forward motion. In the dimness of the morning he could not see any emitting light from the beacon. Lurching, the crawler headed away from the men and instantly blended into the storm. Shep gave a quick eye towards the tethered goats being left behind, then quickly herded the remainder within touch of the crawler.

ELEVEN

Checking the tether and connections to the beacon, Mat strained to peer through the blanket of white. Knowing that Tell, arriving from the west, and the professors from the south east, he worried about the lack of visibility of the beacon. This storm had been raging for several days, with no end between battling warm and cold clashing air. Tell should have been at the compound a day and a half previous. Was Tell unable to see the beacon; bypassed the compound or stopped until visibility returned.

Most early winter quarter seasonal storms were a conflict of normalcy. One moment a blast of passing air would freeze exposed skin, then instantly a wave of warm air forced the removal of mitts and the lifting of the hat's ear flaps. Matt folded up the ear flaps and breeched open the collar of his coat. A strange hum sound filtered through the storm winds and interested his hearing. A low rumbling hum and a click-click sound arrived from an undetermined direction. Immediately, Mat assumed that the compound generator was acting up. Eyes turned towards the barn.

"Stop, Tell, stop," demanded Sally, grabbing Tell's shirt collar, as if the action would quicken the man's reflexes. "That's a mountain wall."

Tell's agitated hands reversed both track levers. Forward motion of the crawler rocked when the dual tracks reversed and clawed into the ground.

"What mountain?" asked Tell, leaning forward to peer through the window. A finger flipped off the power switch. "That my dear companion is the wall of Mat's dome barn."

"We've made it?"

"And, I must say, without doing damage this time, despite weather conditions." A symbolic pat on the back was applied. Tell smiled with pride, relieved that he did not repeat a similar collision as in the previous year. "I will need to find Mat, and the barn's entrance before I move this crawler an inch more."

Mat followed the shadow and winced in anticipation of a collision. 'This has to be Tell.' Mat sighed only when the crawler was entirely inert. A flashback memory from last year flicked in his mind. Tell had stopped short of hitting the home dome only to reverse and compact a fish holding tank. For a week they had fish for lunch and supper.

Rushing forward, Mat approached the side of the crawler, eager to greet a wayward friend. When the door opened to display a stranger, and a female, Mat stepped back with surprise. He did not know what to make of this solid female. It was the reddish braids dangling around a round face of greyish hue, and warm hazel eyes that eased his suspicions of greeting an angry foe.

"This is Tell's crawler," Mat stated rather than asking. "I am Mat."

Her voice responded in a matter-of-fact way. A means to get preliminaries out of the way. "Sally, veterinary. I've accompanied the bovine you requested and is due to calf at any moment. Where is it to be housed?"

Mat's face snickered with blank emotion. A hand raised to point to the dome's opening. "Ah . . ., is there someone . . .?"

"And, I cohabitate with Tell."

Tell's gleaming face bristled with joy from behind a white beard and hair. "Hello . . ., Mat. No damage done this time round."

"Not yet, the entrance is on the other side." Mat gestured without taking eyes from Sally.

"I'll leave that for you to do. I shall introduce Sally to Kat. Ta."

Taking Sally's hand, Tell stepped over the sill and leaped to the ground. "Call us when ready to unload the bovine."

"Nice to meet you," Mat said, his words lost in the wind as the new arrivals inched towards the home dome.

Mat had never envisioned Tell ever cohabitating. It was obvious from Tell's mannerisms and gestures that there was affection for this female. Now that there was another female, would conversations be different? Would Mat be able to get news from afar; practical news of importance, and not fluffy gossip. Climbing into the crawler, he maneuvered the trailer into the barn entrance. Wojo and Bud had sniffed an animal distinction, quite different than local fare.

"Well boys, let's meet our new resident," Mat said to curious companions. "Better stand back, I have no idea what to expect from a bovine."

Unlatching the ramp, a hand began to crank the winch. As the gap between ramp and frame widened, the closer his head advanced, eyes eager to view the creature. He did not know what to expect, what the bovine looked like, and how it would react. Sure, he had seen pictures of various bovines and read up on their temperament. Forty odd years ago, he had actually seen a bovine at a landing compound, a massive beast that continuously rammed its confinement's boundaries. 'Temperamental creatures,' presumed Mat, and expected this one to be of the same attitude.

"You guys had better step back, just to be safe."

Bud backed its hind quarters around the entrance wall. Wojo, eager to do a herding job advanced to the edge of the lowering ramp. Framed by a robust reddish-brown body that seemed to bulge from wall to wall, a white-faced head stretched forward to examine surroundings.

"It is huge, a blimp on four legs."

Wojo's concerned eyes studied the big wide, docile eyes of the bovine. Sensing no immediate danger, Wojo slumped hind haunches. Bud snorted a seemingly approval. Satisfied that there was no need to fear the new accommodations, the bovine sniffed and snorted while a large tongue licked at nostril orifices. Its tongue, a functional testing instrument identified the human, canine, donkey, goats and various foul. What was of interest was a private stall.

"Do I push it out, lead it out, what?" Mat asked Wojo and Bud, and, expected an answer.

Just as Mat's foot lifted to step on the ramp, the crawler rocked. The weight of the newcomer's body extended through an advancing leg and foot placed onto the declining ramp. Slowly the large form waddled down the ramp; paused when close to Wojo and Bud, sniffed a greeting then continued onward.

"Seems friendly," Mat said, and acknowledged Wojo's lifted brow. "It is big, must have four young'ins inside."

As if knowing where to go, the bovine slowly walked, its head turning to inspect the various menagerie and barn objects. Instinct brought the bovine to the section that Mat had set up for the new acquisition. A long tongue grasped up fresh feed before slumping onto its side on the bedding. Tired legs stretched out to recoup from the strain of supporting the extra weight during the long travel duration.

"This has been the easiest farm task I've ever done. Mind you, mind stress can take out just as much energy as a day's work." Bud's head nodded in agreement. Mat often carried out conversations absentmindedly.

Mat and companions, and an odd goat at a time, gathered at the pen rails to observe the new resident. It seemed that the bovine had easily settled in or had the stress of confinement in the crawler been shed out of necessity.

Daydreaming in leisure observation, Mat was oblivious of conversations within the home dome. Instantly after introductions, Kat and Sally felt kindred. As for Tell, the wanderer and deliverer of news was always considered a friend. Tell settled down at the table as Kat began to place out food. Eager to relate gathered news, Tell was silenced by the banter of varied subjects intermingled between the two females. Tell could not enter a word, and had a difficult time trying to make logic of the conversation. A bemused smile creased his lips when realizing that Sally was carrying out a conversation for a duration of ten minutes, which was equal to three days worth of communication between them. Mat entered the dome in mid female chatter. Rarely witnessed to two females carrying on a conversation, he sat mesmerized.

"You do realize that your cohabitator, Tell, is aging," Kat said, a hidden smirk that she and Sally understood. "It is about time he settled down."

The words aging and settle down were the only words understood by Mat and Tell. Heads turned to face each other, and eyes did the scrutinizing. Neither man considered themselves old, but in their view, the other was much older. Tell did have a good eight seasons on Mat, and in Mat's opinion that was a lot. Silently, he agreed with Kat.

"I was planning to return to a southern stock compound. A vet is always in demand," Sally said with contemplation. A glance observed the soft features of Tell behind the full white beard and hair. Their cohabitation contract was left open. She could put an end date for the coming spring season. "Tell should not be travelling alone, he deserves to settle down in one place."

"Our compound stock is growing. Plenty of work for a stock vet." Kat's thoughts were selfish; she sought female companionship. Too many years of mingling with Mat, Tell and the professors left her craving differences.

"I have thought of obtaining a crawler and becoming a servicing vet. With Tell staying put, I could take over the crawler and make this my seasonal destination." A nodding head seemed to confirm a conclusion.

A blank stare on Tell's face turned childish with hints of despair. Others were making life decisions for him, without his consent. Minutely his head swayed from side to side, pleading no to all proposed ideas. In contrast, Mat's head swayed no and nodded yes, a typical male confusion reaction.

"Isn't that a great suggestion Mat?" said Kat with a lilt in her voice.

Feeling the penetration of eyes from Tell and the Females, each with conflicting demands, Mat sniffed the air and stared at the food. "No doubt about it, Kat is a great cook. New dishes from the Oliver cook book. Good, eh Kat. You won't go hungry Tell."

Kat was satisfied that Mat was on the fence yet leaning towards her side. Tell concluded that Mat was a down-right, weakly male and traitor to his gender. Sally only glanced once into Tell's eyes yet noticed the tenderness and affection that she had experienced during cohabitation. She had a decision to make before spring season.

TWELVE

"I take it, that we are lost?" Art attempted to peer through the front window into a blanket of white. "Do you think we should stop until this storm ends?"

Being a first-time traveller into the northern sector, it stands to reason that Art would be apprehensive. Though understanding Art's concerns, Pie continued to alternate the direction of the crawler. He hoped that by chance a glimpse of the beacon would indicate their proximity to Mat's compound. Phil and Story remained relaxed, nit-picking upon subjects from opposing views. Neither seemed worried. Years of aimless travels had taught them that life is a time-line interrupted by segments of adventurous incidents. Eventually and at a random interval, they always seemed to arrive at a determined destination.

"Art, my fellow man, do not worry, we will stumble upon the compound."

"When?"

Pie contemplated before replying, "Every moment is equally distributed at a fifty-fifty outcome."

"Logically disappointing."

"Pessimistically stated. I favour an optimistic point of view." Pie's lips parted slightly, satisfied that Art could not argue against a logic of fifty-fifty odds.

A sudden clank echoed through the crawler's interior. Curious heads turned to the rear portion of the crawler. Pie locked the levers into a brake position and shut down the power to the track gears. If the sound returned, then maintenance problems would not be associated to the mechanics of the crawler.

"Did you commit a 'Tell' maneuver?" Story asked, reflective on the number of incidents Tell had managed to destroy of objects when arriving at Mat's compound. "Despite our absentminded tendencies, we have never had a collision."

"My concerned associates, we were in a forward motion. I am certain that we have been assaulted from behind." Pie pointed accusingly towards the rear wall, anticipating a second reverberation.

Shoulders shrugged off the mysterious bang. When bodies relaxed, another crack sounded against the fibrous shell. Logically, each professor suggested a source of the sound and possible cause.

"An enormous bear, a hungry bear. It smells the pasta in the cooking unit." Phil subconsciously rubbed a gurgling stomach. "I do not wish to share food with an ungrateful creature that would accept our donation then devour us for desert."

Pie's logic scoffed at Phil's suggestion. "We are in a storm. The wind has blown an object against the crawler."

"The same object twice."

No sooner had Story uttered the comment, a louder thud reverberated at the crawler's side.

"And . . ., a third time."

Standing boldly, yet reluctant to approach the side door, Art stated matter-of-factly, and without misgivings, "We have passed through the compound blindly, and this Mat fellow has gained our attention to stop."

"Some-what logical," Pie agreed, though was reluctant to approach the door. "Art, you are standing, and closer to the door."

Pie's unstated suggestion to open the door was resented by Art. A rapid succession of taps on the door sent shivers over body hairs. Art stepped back, suddenly contradictory about following Pie's suggestion.

"Maybe it is not this Mat fellow."

"Art, creatures do not announce themselves." Pie glared at Phil before the professor commented, "Nor do bears. This must be a fellow human."

"Be my guest, go forth and greet this fellow being," Story said, gesturing with a suave sway of an arm and hand.

Braced against the crawler's track, Mac leaned against the compressing wind. Eyes focussed on the door, the slight lever movement of the handle, then the parting space and emitted light from the interior. An occupant's facial features began to fill the opening gap.

"Hello . . ., I'm Mac, party member of a surveying team."

After discarding the bulk of a hood, to present features, Mac waited for the occupant to focus on human features.

"Professor Pie, occupant. Enter."

Reaching a hand down to grasp the stranger's hand, Pie drew him into the comfort of the crawler. Human curiosity returned to the professors after Mac removed a bulky coat. Eyes studied each other before a flood of questions bombarded the man. After introductions, in turn Mac had just as many questions to ask of the professors.

"Please, Professor Story," Pie said addressing his equal. "Being a gather of historical information, lead the way."

"Thank you, Professor Pie."

In the moment of composure, all waited for questions and answers, and in turn addressed Mac. Over time Mac began his questions in search of answers. A history of characters and of timelines, and events were revealed.

"Do you see, Professor Art, being optimistic has been in the surveyor's favour," said Pie, confident of the fifty-fifty rule having a positive outcome.

"By chance, I noticed the crawler when using the lavatory unit," Mac said. "I had just emerged to see a shadowed form passing between the dome and lavatory unit."

Art turned to see Pie's mocking smug grin. "Yes, Pie, the fifty-fifty rule is always in your favour, if always being optimistic."

"Shall we gather in our dome and share a meal. Goat stew and plenty of it."

Mac stood, eager to depart. Turning to the door, Phil was there waiting. A smile of hungry pleasure rose behind excited whiskers.

"Bring our pasta to the feast."

With that statement, Phil pushed the door against the wind and exited into the mixture of warm and cold air. Huddled in a pack, the group headed towards the shadow of the dome. A sweet aroma of warmth filled the dome with the scent of goat stew. The surveyor men were bemused by Mac's find. All were refreshed after several days of recuperation, a change from the image the professors expected after the details of their adventure of survival. Don's sight had begun to clear and objects were cloudy yet recognizable. In a day they would embark south.

After making acquaintances, historical dialogue emerged about each person and missions. When arriving at a current point in time each man rushed to tell news of the shepherd group to the professors. Each burst forth and traipsed over each other's sentences.

"This woman . . .," began Mac.

"One female is this big," Fred said, placing cupped hands in front of his belly.

"I've never seen such a sight . . ., big. She waddles when she walks." Sid swayed from side to side in a lumbering manner.

"I could not see a thing," Don's voice rose above the others. "From the description and deductions, this female, May, is with child, impregnated."

"Pregnant!" clarified Mac.

Each man's head nodded in response to the blank, bewildered stares from the professors. Phil placed inquisitive hands against his own protruding belly.

"Impossible," Story snorted. "No human has been birthed outside of birthing departments on habitats."

"When?" Art asked. "I mean, when will the birthing take place?"

Scratching at tangled hair, Mac squinted. "Ed figures, he knows about goat birthing, and thinks she is due to . . ., pop a baby out soon."

"Impossible," Story reiterated. "Lander females are not capable; their bodies are not suitable. I have seen birthing subjects, large females, wide hips, full breasts to contain nourishment."

Everyone turned to stare with questioning interest.

"Why do you know so much about females and human reproduction? You are a Professor of literature."

"And history, Pie. I gather historical facts about everything."

Stiffening to proclaim authority, Pie stated, "You are not a Professor of medicine. So, it is possible that this May human is capable and able to create a human outside of the birthing department."

Story hesitated in ponder of thoughts, searching through memory files. "If sterilization was missed, both on male and female at puberty, or reversed by a miracle, then possibilities could take a course of action. Centuries ago all females were functioning vessels, though success was variable,"

"Meaning?" Don asked, sensing possible problems.

"Death of the bearer, death of the infant, physical problems in the aftermath to both bearer and infant, and some females were not designed for the process." Story's voice waned when observing concealed expressions in eyes behind the faces of all. "As Pie has indicated, I am not a Professor of medicine, just a collector of facts."

"I am familiar with the artistic aspects of varied females," said Art, seemingly bragging. "Story has stated that a specific birthing bearer has wide hips, and full breasts. Does May have suitable features?"

Each man recalled mind images of their encounter with May. A comparison to Jill was made, yet a defined difference could not be made. Having never seen females of Story's description, they could not produce a clear description.

"We have established that she had a protruding belly," reconfirmed Mac. "Hips were . . .," Extended hands varied in width to express the dimensions of an imaginary hip.

"Breasts were hidden under clothing," Fred confirmed. "She did posses them; they were obviously objects forcing clothing to stretch outwards."

"Yet," interrupted Sid, feeling confident of facts. "I would say that Jill's abundance in anatomy was greater than May. And, she was not pregnant. Is that the right word . . ., pregnant?"

Story nodded confirmation. While the men chatted and expressed their imagination of what May's body resembled unseen beneath clothing, Pie paced.

"May we assume, using a robust stature of Professor Phil as an example, would May resemble proportions?" Pie pointed to plump professor Phil spooning from a second helping of stew.

Instantly heads researched the possible match. They held varied appearing images, and even though May's belly extended, there was an allure of emotion that they did not understand.

"According to professor Story and his description of birthing vessels, we can see that May does not fit a suitable profile. Without knowing birthing statistics from humanities' past, we can conclude that a successful birth will be devastating." Pie's voice trailed to a whisper of disappointment.

Heads drooped, followed by a collective sigh of disappointment. Even Phil expressed sadness by sipping a spoonful of stew very slowly. A sudden burst of wind shuttered the dome. Eyes turned to Pie standing stiffly with a slight grin twitching mustache hair at the corner of his mouth.

"Miracles do happen. We just need to be on the positive side of a fifty-fifty chance. Imagine the birth of a human, a first baby lander growing up in a new birthing world. A potential leader governed by the new earth. The infant shall never know the existence of ocean habitats." Pie's grin grew into a broad smile. "The child will need knowledge to survive beyond infancy," added Pie, a sleeve brushing moisture form a rosy cheek.

"Literature, history, science, the scholastic and social necessities," Story listed, adding on a higher level of knowledge. "Philosophy, mechanics, engineering and culinary ability."

Drawn into the exuberance, the surveyors felt proud to be a part of the birthing process of humanity and of the earth by being messengers of the event. Last to put his worth into the mix, Art stood to forcefully add."

"And, the arts are equally important. This child needs the mentoring of Professors, us! We have a purpose."

Don's low toned voice chilled the moment, "This miracle needs to happen first. We are heading south and will be back in the spring season. I do hope we arrive to bare witness to successful news. We shall hold silent, and not boast of uncompleted news until events are confirmed."

"You shall hear good news." Pie's staunch expression exuding a positive statement.

THIRTEEN

Ed's rested eyes opened. Darkness of night hung over the dome along with a silence. His eyes searched through the interior blackness in search of the source of the silence. The lack of sound was just as disturbing as the continuous wind. 'No wind,' Ed concluded. This storm was over. Confident, he scurried to the door, pushing against a blockage on the exterior. Sand covered with drifting snow had banked against the dome and crawler. A clear night revealed stars twinkling in the heavens and vertical waves of the Aurora- Borealis to the north and above the glacier wall. Twisting in an arc, Ed lowered eyes with each rotation until the light from the beacon fixed his stare.

It was real, bright and inviting. It was then that Ed realized that they had travelled too far northward. Instead of being closer, they were a day further added to their previous calculated distance. They had not gained a closeness. Resenting failure, Ed kicked at the snow and sand mixture banked against the crawler. Frustration of the unknown irritated nerves. He had no idea of May's condition or expected due date. Would delivery be as simple a procedure as a goat?

Digging through the banked sand and snow between the crawler's tracks, he inserted a glow-stick. Eyes of bedded goats shone red against the yellowish light emitted by the glow-stick. Satisfied that his charges were accounted for. Ed marked an arrow into the ground to indicate their direction of travel towards the beacon. An urgency enticed him to push towards the beacon, hoping that other humans were at the location, and possessed knowledge. If travelling continuously night and day, the party should arrive without incidents arising. Now that the storm was over, available energy could be drawn from the sun's light source to power the crawler and bank the storage batteries.

Ed's mind calculated distance; travel speed, and weight capacity of the crawler verses maximum speed per weight ratio. Feeling rested, he would have begun a journey at this moment. Reflecting on others' needs, he crawled back into bed next to May. Two-week-old kids, late arrivals to the herd lay cuddled on top of the sleeping bag next to May's bloated abdomen. In the remaining area, he lay, his mind plotting. 'If I put as many goats as possible into the crawler and run at top speed, the distance could be covered in a day and night. Shep would keep the remaining herd on track. But, running at top speed, the batteries may drain. Run at slow speed and it might take three days to cover the same distance. No . . ., run full speed during the day and slow at night. No . . ., no . . ., bank energy during the day and run at slow speed, then go all out at night. Yes . . ., Shep may trail, but will track and arrive when . . .,' thoughts drifted into a dream world as Ed's eyes closed to savour the rest of the night.

Huddled together on the bench seat of the crawler, Ed pointed to the beacon's light diming as the dawn's sunlight shortened ground shadows.

"That is a reassuring sight," Jill said, hiding her own worrisome thoughts about May. "My weather calculations indicate, clear conditions. Good for visibility, though clarity will bring ever dropping nighttime temperatures."

"Maybe just one night of fighting the cold," Ed suggested, eyeing a possible reaction from May.

Both Jill and Ed waited for a comment. Without turning heads, eyes rolled towards May sitting in the centre placement on the hard bench. Continuously munching on dried bread, she seemed content and complacent on a down-filled sheep shearling hide. Ed and Jill's eyes moved to the large belly then to question each other. Both had the same knowledge concerns; lack of human birth experience, and an urgency to arrive at a location where possible help might be. Seemingly they had concluded a similar tactic. Both voices spoke, and words were disregarded by May.

"We go all out."

Ed's hands unlocked the track levers. The crawler rocked under the weight of the payload of goats. Once in motion the assemble jostled for reclining space. Shep urged the remaining herd into motion. Sensing an urgency, the herd-dog began to advance the rested herd in advance of the slow-moving crawler.

Delighted by the rocking of the crawler, May sensed a peacefulness within the belly. Though the motion was soothing for her body, it was the mind that grew agitated. Thoughts argued about what-ifs? Lack of knowledge and the human experience concerning conception; development, birthing and rearing during a first-time participation, a learn as-you-go process. In a way the process had been natural and was taking care of itself. It was the future points of the process that worried May, the unknown. Birthing; would there be pain, how does a human deliver, what is to be done, feeding, when, how often, excrement removal, growth, care and teaching? An internal sweat felt cool against cold weather clothing. Beads of sweat on her forehead would be noticed by Jill and Ed.

'If they notice, they will be worried and anxious. And, that will make me worried.' May's thoughts were active and lively within. Stanch and restrictive nerves kept the body from reacting in similarity to thoughts. With a casually raised arm, she dabbed at beads of sweat gathering on eyebrows. When sticking a piece of dried bread into her mouth, jill and Ed would not take any notice of visual anxiety. 'Can't this crawler go any faster. I could out-walk it, even in my overly plump . . ., no . . ., fat condition.'

As if hearing unspoken words, Ed turned to study May's face. A smile of companionship's warmth pushed up flushed cheeks on May's face. Ed returned a manly, nothing-wrong smile.

May's sarcastic thoughts wanted to demand that Ed force the track levers into a second advanced notch.

Also seeking the guidance of the beacon, though never rushed, the Professors let their crawler advance on a selected course. Mundane activities occurred along with continual and random conversations on various topics. Though random glances were made through the window for the tell-tale sighting of the beacon, they knew that a daylight sighting would be nil. Assumptions were that the crawler was heading in a correct direction, so visual observations were not made to encompass a three-hundred and sixty-degree view. At the day's end all eyes gathered at the window in search of the beacon's light.

Requesting fresh air, Art opened the side door and swallowed cool evening nourishment. The sudden coolness watered eyes forcing Art to blink rapidly. A kaleidoscope of colours formed on moisture crystals across the pupils of the eyes. Fascination of colour intrigued the Professor of the arts; for such refraction of colour required a singular source of light. Wanting the display to continue, Art leaned further out into the coolness and blinked. Unfortunately, the eyes cleared to reveal a singular light source.

"Professors?" Art called out, retaining a fix on the glow on the horizon. "What is this beacon light's description?"

"Globe in shape with yellowish light," Pie replied.

"Yes, though as if a twinkling star fell from the heavens."

"A perfect rendition, Professor Phil," praised Pie, leaning closer to the window in expectation of seeing the descriptive beacon.

Widening eyes to clear away moisture, Art stated, "I do believe we are heading in the wrong direction. The crawler is heading south-west. If this is the beacon of your description, then it is located north-east."

Deserting the front window, Professors Pie, Phil and Story crowded the narrow opening of the door. Instantly the cool night air's crystallization of moisture on their eyes produced prisms of colour. Eyelids blinked, and minds registered the enjoyment of the visual colour spectrum. Briefly the visions remained then vanished to leave behind the distinctive reflection of the beacon's glow.

"Yes, Art, that is Mat's beacon," Phil concluded. "Ever faithful it glows to guide the lost, the seekers, and wayward Professors that should be mindful of being absentminded of daily necessities."

"Insightful observation," said Pie, eyes squinting in thought. "We do tend to spend too much time discussing and debating than attending to functional chores."

Rubbing a hand over a gurgling belly, Phil nodded in agreement. "That said, did we prepare an evening meal?" Phil's eyes closed with an effort to remember earlier events.

Story added with conviction, "I believe we discussed making a thick pudding. Undecided on who would make it, we then argued about the required ingredients, be it dessert based, or protein based."

"My conclusion was dessert based," Phil reaffirmed.

"Pie's eyes and cheeks puffed into a smile. "At the last vote, I believe the count was three to one in favour of dessert-based pudding, and though Art desired protein based, he should be punished and voted maker of the pudding."

Feeling the weight of associates leaning against him at the door, Art leaned inward and pulled the door closed. "As has been stated, we have again become absentminded."

"How so?" demanded Phil, his hand attempting to settle a growling stomach. "We have missed a meal . . .."

"And, agreed on dessert," added Story.

"You, professor Art was elected to make the pudding dessert," confirmed Pie, pleased to conclude the discussion of importance.

Drawing hands down his face, elongating frustrated features, Art's distorted eyes glared at the bewildered Professors. "I do believe we have located the beacon in question. Rather than adjust the crawler's direction . . ., pudding is of more importance."

Phil's grumbling stomach made clear its desire. Admonishing eyes turned to gang up on the Professor, knowing what he would say.

"A course correction," Pie stated, heading to the controls.

Faces lingered at the window until the beacon's light reflected in the centre of the direction marker etched into the window. Satisfied by the course correction and of the speed of the crawler, three Professors reclined and stared innocently at Professor Art.

"What?" Art questioned, as if being accused of inappropriate manners. "Fine . . ., I will make the pudding . . ., dessert pudding."

Smiling faces were accompanied by Phil's gurgling stomach.

FOURTEEN

Anxious faces crowded the viewing surface of the crawler's window. A hint of disappointment lingered in their scanning eyes. Pie slowed the crawler into the lowest gear ratio, as if not wanting to approach the compound. Desertion of the compound seemed to be evident. No activity was visible on the grounds. Usually Wojo would be slumbering in the middle of the pathway. When hearing an approaching crawler, the hound would lazily greet with a forced lift of the head. The hound was not in sight, nor the donkey, Bud, a menacing beast that Phil disliked. For some unknown reason the two did not like each other.

Sporadic dust devils skirted across the compound expressing a desertion of occupants. Garden utensils rested upright at the end of a half-harvested row of pumpkin. Eyes darted to the slight rotation of a water windmill and to Tell's crawler, its tracks banked by snow and sand. The grey coloured bulk resembled a weather-beaten relic of a previous century.

"The place is deserted!" Art started to say, disappointed by the compound's appearance, and of the descriptive hype the other professors gave of their winter refuse. "Only the beacon seems to be the only occupant."

Pie disengaged the forward motion of the crawler at walking distance from the centre of the compound. All remained at the window, their eyes gravitating to every motionless object and detail of the compound.

"Something is amiss," Pie said, revealing a theory of anarchy, then expressed positivity. "I believe it to be the midday . . ., yes, it is feeding time. Everyone has gathered to eat; humans in the house dome and animals in the barn dome."

"Yes . . ., yes . . .," the Professors exclaimed, ridding thoughts of devastation and self-induced thoughts of horror. Art was the exception, for this was a first visitation to the compound and of meeting inhabitants. Though the presentation of this remote compound was visibly bland and deserted, the artistic side of Art's makeup did see the beauty of rustic simplicity.

"Remaining here will not solve any riddle of the unknown," quipped Story.

Taking initiative, his smallness of stature squeezed past robust Phil and lanky Pie. Art hopped eagerly behind, somewhat unsure about wanting to follow second in line or tag along behind Phil and Pie. An odd silence greeted the quartet upon debarking the crawler. Strong wind sounds of the storm lingered in their memory, they would have to adjust ears to the quietness. Acute ears listened for minute sounds of existence; of humans, animals, even the faint sound of an insect just to prove that there was life.

Placing a foot down then pausing before advancing, the professors ghostly advanced. First the garden then a water tank was passed until their bodies were able to lean forward towards the barn dome's entrance. Necks stretched, and heads turned acutely to face the glow of interior light. Eyes widened to see goats in recline and milling lazily. Phil's eyes noticed the dangerous hind legs and whitish-black rump of the disliked donkey.

"That donkey is alive?" Phil said, a hint of disappointment in a non-pleasing tone.   "It seems that all animals are . . .," Story's mind searched for a positive word that would not indicate their thoughts of finding every creature dead. "normal."

Relieved of tension; breathing returned to normal, legs relaxed, and tense shoulders slumped. Standing upright with ease, their eyes upon the backs of human occupants of the compound gathered and attentive to a commotion within a stall.

"Our hosts," Pie said to Art, casually indicating the humans as if their fears were trivial. "I shall introduce you to our friends."

Pie brazenly led the way into the dome and through the parting goats. Bud and Phil locked eyes and instantly animosity in both flamed. Seeking protection, Phil buffeted the distance by placing Art and Story between.

Obviously, some action of interest held Kat, Mat and Tell's attention to objects inside of the stall. Even Wojo had to observe, its head resting on a rail, and body in a relaxed prone position.

As if being expected, the approach of the professors did not startle the residents. Bodies gathered, in close proximity, sensed the forms of the professors leaning over a stall rail to observe with interest. Eyes darted from face to face and heads acknowledged greetings and introductions.

"Pie," "Tell," "Phil," "Miss Kat," "Mat," "Tell," "Art?" "Mat," "Art," "Kat."

Having made the rounds of acknowledgement and leaving no one unaccounted for, there came a pause of silence. The pause allowed the new arrivals to witness the object of interest inside of the stall.

"That is a bovine," Phil indicated, then realized that the animal would be known to all. "I mean to say . . ., is the bovine sick?"

Kat's face brightened into a smile. "No, she is pregnant and is about to deliver."

"And who is that person . . ., and what is she doing?" asked Story, observing the woman with arm extended into the genitals of the bovine. A painful frown twisted his lips.

"Oh, I am ashamed of my lack of manners." Tell extended an open hand to the woman and the other to the professors. "May I introduce Sally. Sally these are the professors; Pie, Phil, Story and a new added professor . . ., Art."

Curious of why the woman was penetrating the prone bovine, Pie leaned towards Tell to ask, "What is she doing?" his voice echoed for all to hear.

Not just one answer was given.

"Sally is a vet," Tell stated flatly, an inner pride widened a slight smile.

"I acquired a bovine to stock the farm," Mat concluded.

"A doctor!" in the back of his mind, Pie concluded that a doctor was a doctor regardless of the patient . . ., whether animal or human. "I have a pain in my ankle, would Sally be willing ti inspect?"

Tell's blank expression was lost to Pie's intent.

Questioning the procedure, which looked painful to the lowing bovine, Story inquired, "Is this the standard procedure required to deliver an offspring?"

"Sally says," Kat began, her eyes and emotion fully concentrated on the labouring bovine. "this will be the first calf, and the mother needs a bit of assistance."

Strangely in unison, as if the minds of the professors were linked upon the same thought, leaned heads back to exchange glances of despair.

Story mumbled words before expressing a full question to Kat, "Would this actual procedure be required upon a human female in a state of deliverance of a human calf for the first time?"

Confused and astonished by Story's question, Kat's mind reeled for memory facts. She had to admit to herself of never witnessing a human birth or having read or studied the facts. Human births on ocean habitats was contained in the birthing department. Though knowing its location when growing up and having the realization that the department was not secret or restricted; life at that time frame had no interest. Having such a question asked, she herself wondered if human delivery was intoxicating to witness as it was painful for the bovine? In her mind she envisioned human birthing mothers in the birthing department crying out in pain as attendants pried out a baby. Shivers tickled behind ears at the thought that she was birthed in a similar way and caused such pain to a birthing host.

Turning a sombre expression to be greeted by Story's same reflection, Kat's voice cracked, "I don't know . . ., I would hope not."

Both turned heads back to the unfolding scene when Sally's husky voice drew everyone's attention. "Here come the front hooves, and I see a pink nose."

Mouths of viewers gapped, hands tightened upon the gate rail, eyes widened. Kat braved outward emotion, yet moisture flowed from eye ducts. Tell's head rested on crossed arms laying on the rail, a strange sensation of emotion drew him closer to the essence of Sally, beyond being proud of her ability and talent. For the professors, vessels for gathering knowledge and in turn to each other, they inhaled each minute detail.

With hands grasped onto the calf's two front hooves, Sally braced legs against the bovine's rump. She waited for the bovine to relax and take in a deep breath. When the bovine was ready to push, Sally tugged to add assistance. Tension seemed to stall then the bovine sucked in air; its stomach collapsed, and hips relaxed. With a final effort of a push, Sally pulled the calf free. The birth sack covered the calf's nose and mouth preventing any indication of breathing. Onlookers held their breaths. Sally's fingers quickly cleared nostrils and throat then hands massaged the wet belly. A gasp and snort by the calf cleared the air passages and instantly the calf came to life.

Witnesses were privileged to see the instant moment of life, that spark that kickstarted existence. Tragically in this moment non-existence could have played out. Though Mat and Kat had previously witnessed goat births, this birth was just as magical and heartwarming. For Tell and the professors, having viewed the birthing of life, they were overwhelmed and could not disguise smiles and tears. Manly behavior would be forgiven at an ecstatic moment as this.

Quickly, Sally moved the female calf within reach of the mother to lick clean; to taste, to add scent and familiarity, a bonding process that links a mother and calf. All watched, spellbound, only Sally noticed that something was wrong when she tried to urge the bovine to rise. Though breathing and heartbeat had been elevated during delivery, the bovine's stats were back to normal, it was the lack of strength in the hind quarters that she noticed. Fearing a pelvic dislocation, she began an exploratory examination. Mesmerized eyes accompanied by expressive uhs . . ., and ahs . . ., from the gallery upon the calf did not focus on Sally and her trepidation. A bovine that could not stand to carry on normal functions and milk would waste away, as would its calf.

Pressing hands around a back quarter and rotating to test for flexibility, an eye caught the soft texture of another hoof emerging from the bovine's vagina.

"Another calf!" Sally squealed, a high-pitched voice that was not reminiscent of her normal low tone. "A twin!"

"Where?" asked Art, leaning childishly over the railing. If allowed, he would be at Sally's side, an annoyance in an exuberance to experience life's wonders.

"Right here," replied Sally, assuming an assistance position behind the bovine.

The bovine was tired, drained of strength from the first birth. It was imperative that the calf come out quickly, even if the bovine did not want to assist.

"Mat," Sally said with urgency. "I need you and a rope."

A flash of movement was all the bystanders viewed as Mat retrieved Bud's lead rope and scrambled over the rails and into the stall. With a loop fashioned, Sally's large hand pushed the rope into the vagina and fastened it over a pair of hooves.

"When I say pull, Mat, pull. We will have one opportunity. I would say that the bovine only has one push left."

Mat and Sally gripped the rope and added a bit of tension. Their legs bent and braced ready to extend explosively. Sally watched the rise and fall of the stomach, and the licking action of the tongue upon the calf. The tongue retracted; nose snorted, and a breath was held. At that moment Sally noticed the stomach force muscles to push, she gave the order.

"Pull . . .,"

With moral support onlookers pulled with grins and body animation. Mat and Sally pulled and attempted to extend legs. For a moment nothing happened. A suck sound of air expelling was heard and at that moment, Mat and Sally drew the calf fully out. Greeting them was the weak bellow of the calf.

A grouped ahh . . ., resounded arousing Wojo. The hound glanced over the rail then returned to a prone position.

"A bull calf," Sally announced, her drained strength attempting to move the large calf within reach of the mother.

Shaking his head slowly from side to side, Story seemed perturbed. "Is this the way a human is delivered?"

Collectively, the professors turned to face each other, their minds contemplating. Kat and Tell quickly turned to question Story's odd question.

"A human?" Tell asked, intrigued by the odd inquiry of human birthing.

"What human?" Kat's voice carried a tone of worry and excitement, an inner sensation unexplainable. Human birthing did not exist outside of birthing departments, so why would such a subject be brought up?

Mat and Sally gathered at the rail while individual mumbling commenced. Mat's calm demeanour intervened.

"There is a fascinating turn of events that the professors are privy to. I trust that Professor Story will enlighten us with details?"

FIFTEEN

Merriment commenced during the evening meal within the main dome. Having accommodated themselves for the winter quarter season in respective smaller domes, the Professors, Tell and Sally gathered to feast on Kat's prepared meal. Though the found cookbook; its location of being found, was of interest and of the recipes that Kat had tried and currently prepared, all dwelled on the birth of the calves and of human birth.

"We should go searching for the group," suggested Tell, eager to venture out with Mat.

Past excavations, and wanderings by the pair, was a bonding matter after separated for three-quarters of the year. This part of the year held change for Tell, having shared intimacy and emotions with Sally. Yet, there is a need to be with Mat exploring remains of a physical past. Afterall, Tell was the deliverer of news from settlement to settlement. News of a human birth would be the most important incident during his existence. He could not wait for the occurrence to find him, he needed to seek out the source first hand.

In the back of his mind a voice continued to suggest remaining in one location. Age had suddenly, it seemed over the past year or so, to slow movement down. Time is always continuous, yet Tell's ability of body functions had slowed. He had mellowed; has put more thought into situations and enjoyed the pace of existing. A smile of pride and satisfaction glowed in eyes and on cheeks when thinking of the duration of sensuality spent with Sally. Evenings of intimacy lasted ten times longer than a youthful splurge. The down side of thoughts was a question of, 'would Sally renew their cohabitation contract or just extend the duration through their return trip south in the spring quarter'.

Tell's voice hinted at an urgency, "The female could be in distress?"

"She might be," Sally's voice stated between suggestions of trying several recipes with Kat. "Beef is of suitable taste, but it will be some time before a herd is sustainable for harvest."

"Beef Wellington," Phil slobbered the words as past thoughts of the devouring teased taste buds. "Many, many years ago . . ., oh to experience such taste."

"If there are complications, I am of no assistance," Sally's tone had not changed between the discussion of recipes and of human birth. Just facts were being stated.

Pie paced around the table seemingly lost in thought, as he continuously filled, refilled and toped up mugs with hot tea. The strong aroma of the wild harvested pant wafted through the dome. "Unfortunately, we professors have knowledge in unrelated fields. My dear Miss Sally, you are gifted with talent and medical knowledge that is relatively available." A lanky arm filled Sally's mug to the brim with tea.

"Close is not close enough." Though a tough presence encompassed her external form, there was a shakiness of fear in her words.

"Mat," Pie shouted, having a eureka moment of thought. "Where did you find this cookbook?"

Startled by the professor's voice, Mat glanced to individual faces of surprise and questions intended to interrogate. A finger waved a point of direction to the west face of the dome's wall. Not liking to be the centre of attention, Mat stuttered with a tendency to deny finding the cookbook.

"Ah . . ., over there." With reference an arm and hand forced a finger to indicate a location only known to himself. "There are ruins at the top of the plateau where the glacier compacted structures against a mountain. I've been exploring deeper and deeper into various structures and came to an archive, maybe a museum of sorts, or an ancient library."

"Where knowledge can be found," Pie's words were a statement of fact rather than a question put forth to Mat.

"The cookbook is one of a kind," Kat said, while eyes of green sparkled with childish lust. Pinkish skin flushed a change of tone as she and Sally exchanged a personal secret. "Mat has brought back what is known as romance novels, quite titillating."

"Yes, I've read a passage from, 'Miss Chatterley's Lover'. The . . ., what did you say it was . . ., yes a paperback romance." The grey tone of Sally's skin colour did not alter tones, yet a lilt of giddiness in the voice intrigued Tell.

The visual complexities of body expressions were not obvious to Pie, his concern was on books . . ., books that contained knowledge. "In a library of a reference archive there are books of knowledge. All you need to do, Mat, is find a reference book of human medical knowledge. Thus, Miss Sally will read and . . ., I will be confident in saying that we all will master the birthing process in a human. If . . ., if I say, a complication arises, we will be able to find a solution."

Intruding on the gaiety of the gathering and halting voices in mid speech, a loud thud resounded from the dome entrance door. Startled eyes turned towards the sound, an unnatural sound. Frozen in statuette pose, the gathered subjects waited, their minds abundant with questions and assumptions.

All were present, all familiar to one-another. Accustom to cohabitation, no-one present would bother to knock. Freedom to open any door and announce themselves was acceptable. A loud knock vibrating through the door had startled the assembled into submissiveness.

"Has the wind picked up and cast an object against the door," suggested Story, his hands grasping securely to the table edge.

Body actions varied individually, yet all had a fear of the sudden unknown source of the sound.

"It's that donkey . . ., Bud," Phil claimed, well-aware that the donkey had yet to assault him upon arrival. "That brute had not attacked me yet . . . and is now in pursuit."

"Really, Phil?" Pie said, scoffing at the ridiculous assumption Phil proposed. "Would a donkey introduce its arrival?"

"Something is at the door," replied Phil, slumping at the table, a hand comforted by a selection of food.

"Mat!"

"Yes, Kat?"

"Don't be foolish, go see what the problem is."

"Me?"

"As compound facilitator, you hold representation."

Kat's hand lifted Mat's elbow, a slight gesture of commanding him to comply. Stiffly, without confidence, Mat rose and edged forward. A second rap echoing from the door forced Mat to drag a foot until a succession of light rapping sounds sounded humanly friendly.

"Obviously a human unaccustomed to our open-door policy."

With confidence, Mat rushed to the door. Not to prolong curiosity, the unlatched door was quickly opened wide. Framed under the arched frame, three unknown humans blocked the view of the compound. Instantly, resident eyes gravitated to the round protruding belly of a female prudently positioned between associates. Fascination of the oddity consumed the combined thoughts of the residents. All displayed frozen facial features of bewilderment by the strangeness of the human deformity.

"It's them," Pie proclaimed with hands extended as if ready to support the large protrusion. "The pregnant Female."

"Manners, Pie," Kat whispered, standing in front of Pie, anticipating that the professor might do something foolish with his extended hands. It was possible for the intelligent man to foolishly and inappropriately touch the female.

At the same instant, Sally stood to accompany Kat towards the weary pregnant female. Compassionately, Kat and Sally catered to the female, removing coat and escorting her to a seat at the table. Voices chorused with introductions, questions and instructions while being overly accommodating.

Briefly rising to whisper to Tell, Sally demanded, "I need a human medical reference book."

Filled with purpose, Tell straightened, determined to comply with Sally's demand. Backing to stand by Mat, Tell whispered. "I have been ordered to find a medical book. You, my friend, will lead the expedition."

"I guess we should leave now. She is ready to burst." Mat began to back towards the door as if escaping from an expected explosion. "How . . ., big is . . ., the human inside? Is this normal?"

Mat and Tell backed out through the door, pressing through side by side. Drawing the door closed to block the interior view, the pair breathed with relief, as if safely removed from potential complications.

SIXTEEN

Meandering across the flatlands without an intent to exert themselves, Mat and Tell were lost in their own thoughts. The magnitude of the storm had been forgotten when enjoying the cool windless day. Obstacles of indifference were small windswept ridges of sand and snow hardening under the cooling temperature of the winter season. Sensing a distance half way to the mountain, Mat turned to sight in the beacon. Though servicing before leaving, a constant check on the functioning light secured faith for a safe return.

Having mingled through various areas of the crushed structures pressed against the north face of the mountain, ninety percent still awaited inspection. By his account, Mat calculated that a better part of a city had been pressed against the mountain by the south bound glacier. An amazing result was that some interior rooms of the buildings were fairly intact, while others were compacted ruble. Mat had no fear of the unknown when exploring and excavating. Discovering the undiscovered answered questions about the past history of human civilization, and also confused the mind. How did an intellectual civilization with a mindset of superiority and dominance succumb to eradication? Over confidence can be a weakness.

The physical world was not feared; inanimate objects were such, harmless, wild animals dangerous, yet understood and complied with as necessary. It is the human mind when allowed to wander that creates fear. At times, Mat had rested within the compressed rooms of ruble and heard noises, faint-like voices. Then the mind created images of human deformed caricatures and a society of demonic beings that survived earth's destruction by mutating. At moments like this, he would vow not to read those science-fiction paperbacks, yet when finding a new one, devour each page with enthusiasm. Fiction is fiction and the reality of earth's destruction did not allow for such nonsense of fabricated fiction.

Never rushing, nor taking chances within the mountain, Mat allowed the years of exploration to drag on. Small discoveries had been made, as in the finding of the cookbook, but a larger discovery may be buried deeper into the ruble. Pressure to find a medical reference book is an undaunting task, even a ridiculous request. Mat squinted and contorted facial features into a dejected mask. This request was too much, in too little of time, and in a dangerous and unexplored location.

From behind, Tell noticed Mat's head swaying and shoulders hunching. From experience, Tell knew when Mat was in deep thought. Nervously turning, Tell blinked at the sight of the beacon. He was glad to tag along behind Mat, a man familiar with the land and of the movement on foot. If residing here under the companionship of the beacon, Tell felt inclined to enjoy a peaceful existence. There is a difference between walking the landscape in a comfortable crawler and braving existence on foot and facing nature face to face. Tell's mind gravitated to a singular-one-place residence. A lifetime of visual images, locations, destinations and human contacts was enough. Tell craved relaxation. Wandering behind Mat and not having to think, worry or strain was now, and would be a pleasure to experience in the future. Ninety-nine percent of his mind was made up, he would be staying put here at the compound. A suggestion would be made to Sally. If the hoped-for result was negative, then the crawler would be at her disposal.

"We'll rest here and have tea and stew," Mat said, sitting on a log facing the beacon.

Drawn out of thought, Tell wondered were the time had gone? The walk was a blink in time. From the plateau of the mountain, the beacon stood out below and at a distance. "Wow, we are far. The beacon is a welcoming soul of existence, drawing humanity to a source of companionship and fruition."

"Planning on becoming a professor with such statements of intellect?"

"No, Mat, but think of this. The beacon has brought me with news and gossip of the world; Sally with knowledge of animals and stock health, the professors with knowledge of the sciences and arts, Kat, our agriculturist, and you, out compound coordinator, archeologist and the man that provides shelter and caretaker of the beacon."

"A mighty mouthful." Mat's reaction humorous over the humble gratitude of the honor placed upon him. "I prefer rancher and part-time explorer."

"Yes, yes, all secondary." Tell was on a roll, feeling inspired by the grandeur of the vista and the stimulation of the trek. "And now you are host to a shepherd, a meteorologist and a geologist. Not to mention the witness of a . . ., a . . ., what do we call it, a newer version of humanity, a first human born on land by natural . . . means."

Mat's head drooped with despair. Hands busied with heating the tea and stew over a portable stove. "I think the natural, old world way is a dangerous gamble. Too many things can go wrong. Goats, sheep, dogs and wildlife have been doing the breeding and delivering components continuously. Mankind halted the natural way and developed a breeding practice to unify all races into a mixed species by means of the birthing hosts. Thus, we have become sterile eunuchs and have lost the ability to conceive, gestate and birth."

"Mat," Tell began to boast. "a miracle has happened to landers, ones just like us."

"Sorry, Tell," Mat sipped the warming stew. "old guys like us? No miracle has happened to us. Why this young couple? Maybe something has gone haywire and this will not be a joyous miracle. Like I hinted at; animals have been self-creating continuously and yet, fetuses have been aborted, there are still-births, host mothers dying and young just not surviving through infancy."

Tell's enthusiasm waned. Slumping onto the log, a hand accepted a tea and cup of stew. "You kind of put a damper on the miracle of life."

"Just being realistic. I would like to experience a miracle too, but . . .."

"But what? Think positively. We just concentrate on finding a medical book and apply our abilities towards success." Tell sipped the stew. "Good stew. One point on the positive side of our venture."

A smile creased Mat's lip. "Okay, a good start."

From an overview, the mountain resembled similar natural formations. Mountain formations over time were created by tectonic plates overlapping and pushing formations upward. Weathering winds and rain contoured a plateau before sculptured by an ice-age advancement. What Mat and Tell viewed was a second sculpting by the advancement and retreat of a second ice-age glacier. This time civilization's structures were pushed then pressed against the mountain and plateau. In nature's way of rejuvenation, a blanket of rocks and earth covered man-made structures, hiding the ruins from sight.

Standing before a cave entrance, Mat retrieved two capes from a pack. Handing a poncho style cape to Tell, Mat flicked on the solar lights embedded into the full surface of the capes. Solar storage energy turned the pair into a human glow stick.

"Ready, Tell?"

Tell nodded, though unsure if he would be calm within the bowels of a mountain. As a lander, he was accustomed to the openness of the landscape.

"Who made the cave?" Tell questioned, a means to divert his own thoughts away from entering a confined enclosure.

"A natural occurrence. Glacial run-off carved an opening, a means of releasing water pressure. It also cleared debris from man-made structures buried against the north face of this mountain."

Upon entering the darkness of the cave, the capes' illumination functioned at peek efficiency. Having the brightness illuminating the area as if equal to natural light of the outdoors, Tell's fear subsided.

"This way Tell. I found the cookbook in an entrance way to a much larger opening. Time was limited, so I did not explore further."

"You assumed the area to be a museum or an archive?"

"Just guessing. There were words on a wall, most were destroyed and removed. I did guess at a word, 'depository'."

"Meaning, an archive . . ., maybe a book depository."

"Possibly. Maybe a library or a legal depository archive. This is in a general area where I have gathered books, paperbacks. There is obviously damage due to the crushing and compression, yet glacial water seems to have flowed quickly and over the exterior of the structures."

"A preserved find. We may have good luck."

"We will find out when entering the depository."

After walking on the polished surface of rock beside a trickling stream of glacial water, the men reached a raised platform of steel construction. Protruding from the rock, the structure was odd, out of place; identifiably man-made. Mounting the platform, Mat indicated the descending iron ladder.

"This is the entrance to our ancestor's past."

Peering down, Tell could not see an end. Their light bounced off a void of darkness.

"I believe this to be the roof of a building. I am guessing the bottom to be below the surface of the flatlands."

Tell's eyes squinted, expressing a tiredness of the journey so far. "We have just climbed over three-hundred feet and now need to descend that distance on a rung ladder?"

Grabbing a hand hold on the curved ladder guides, Mat began to descend. Shoulders shrugged off Tell's inference of depth. "I have not reached the bottom. The first areas I've explored are only fifty-feet down."

Only the movement of their bodies and feet against the metal rungs provided natural sounds to their present sanity. Haunting sounds reverberated at intervals, echoing up from the depths. Movement of rock grinding minutely against man-made structures squeaked and dripping water thudded a drum beat of doom.

"Just sounds," Mat reassured Tell, knowing that these new sound experiences would play havoc with rational thoughts. "These sounds affected me the first time I entered this tube. Nothing more than everyday normal earth sounds enhanced by the tube's acoustics."

Remaining silent, Tell stiffened to ward off childish fears. An eagerness wished for a quick exit. "How much further?"

"We're here."

With an extended foot, Mat forced a grotesquely deformed steel door open then stepped onto a slanted floor. Tell anxiously followed. Wide corridors led off in multiple directions. Luminescent particles embedded in the walls reflected their body light as if interior lights had been turned on. Being virgin to the sight of the archive find, Tell marvelled at finding books scattered on the floor, paintings askew on the walls, chairs, tables and unidentified trinkets. Each object was catalogued into his mind for future discussion.

Moving along one passageway in a selected direction, Mat had not yet explored, he gave commentary on previous finds and areas explored. This passage is where the cookbook had been found, though he had not ventured further towards wide double doors with opaque glass.

"I think there is a large room beyond those doors, though no idea what is beyond."

Moving confidently, Mat stepped clear of what seemed to be garbage articles. Unlike previous areas that had organization, as if left untouched when humans abandoned the building, this area was cluttered with waste. Empty food containers with brand name packaging and abused food preparation vessels lay in heaps. Tell and Mat read in silence; 'Boston Pizza, Dominos Pizza, Tim Hortons Tim-Bits, Subway, Bulk Foods, Cosco . . ., Dairy Queen?' Just words on articles that both men had no idea of their meaning or purpose. Having no reference to compare, they discarded the garbage when standing in front of the doors.

Bewildered by the construction of the openings, Mat and Tell searched for handles, hinges and a means of entering through the slab barrier. Attempting to peer into the room through the glass, Tell brushed a sleeve against the glass. A thick cake of grim on the inside prevented a clear vision through.

"This door baffles me," Tell concluded by pressing hands flat against the doors and pushing. "Do you think they slide apart?"

Nodding with agreement, Mat selected a flat piece of steel trim from the junk pile. Forcing the flat sides between the doors, Mat began to lever. Tell added his share of force. Grime of age resisted to a point then the doors gave way. With hands on opposite doors, Mat and Tell forced the doors apart. A dry smell of decay trapped for centuries wafted into nostrils.

Edging into the opening, their body light began to illuminate the room. As if normal, eyes encompassed the entire room then darted to specifics, then to details. Instantly, Mat brought a sleeve to cover his nose and mouth. Drawing a cloth from a pocket, Tell mirrored covering actions. Both men stepped back across the door's threshold.

A history of human life to the end unfolded in their minds as eyes focused on minute details of objects in the large room. Human skeletons lay side by side and end to end over the entire floor. Clothing lay shredded over dry brittle bones. Starvation being the likely cause of their demise. With habitat shrinking and cold becoming unbearable, humans gathered to slowly die. Cannibalism possible. Rodents of all spices gathered where humans resided and waited their turn to feast. When supply was devoured, the rodents in turn became fair game until starvation turned their bodies into skeletons to lay mingled among human counterparts. Lastly, insects became the dominant species, until their nourishment ceased to exist. Bitter cold and suffocation by layers of snow, they became encased by the compression of glacial forces. All manner of life that existed became entombed here in a room beneath a mountain on the flatlands adjacent to Mat's compound.

Without uttering a word or sound, like minds of Mat and Tell had concluded that the doors would be closed, sealing a historical fact. For the time-being they would not discuss this find. Refusing to turn their backs, they backed along the corridor until reaching another adjacent hallway.

"A museum is this way," Said Mat, his voice cracking from clenched vocal chords.

"Where there is a museum is an archive containing books." Tell's tone of voice was attempting to be positive, lighthearted and encouraging.

SEVENTEEN

Images of animated skeletons flashed in Tell's thoughts. Throughout an entire life, Tell recalled only a single occasion when viewing a corpse. A decaying human lay beside a seldom used trail, a trail that he had randomly taken. Beyond recognition and without identification of the being, Tell took time to burry the human and mark the site. Over the years he contemplated upon the human, a life, death and a legacy unknown. The sight of the decaying remains had never bothered him. Today, the moment of experiencing the tomb of skeletons had bothered him. Trailing behind Mat, Tell's mind forced him to glance behind, a defensive means to make sure those skeletons were not following with an intent to pounce. The logic of knowing that the dead do not rise and do not seek vengeance upon the living, could not compete against a vivid imagination.

Annoyed by the constant head turning by Tell, Mat waited until the man's head was facing fully forward before shouting. "Boo . . .!" Mat Gurgled, a low tone rising from deep in the throat.

Tell's face turned ashen, blending ghostly behind the pure white of hair and beard. Pressing his back against the corridor wall, wide eyes accused Mat of poor childish behavior. "Mat . . ., why?"

"Why not?" Mat shrugged shoulders. Decently, he did not laugh or admonish the man. "Just needed to jump start the logical part of your brain. See, no skeletons following, no spirts."

Tell's head remained fixed, only eyes strained to look back down the empty corridor. "I know, it was my idle mind working overtime. And . . ., it is still partially your fault for giving me that book to read . . ., 'The Walking Dead'."

"Those stories can sure stimulate an idle imagination. The mind can be your worst enemy, far worse than what reality has to offer."

"I am going to read that other book . . ., 'Anne of Green Gables'."

A soft laugh resounded from Mat as he recalled the story. "You should have read that one before this excavation."

Leading the way, Mat approached a stairwell. Taking a quick glance down the hallway, Tell breathed in confidence then followed. A strange smell drifted up the stairwell, an odour of dryness, an end result of damp organic paper products drying from an earlier decomposition caused by water and mould. The smell instantly recognizable to the odour of the cookbook and paperback books that Mat had collected.

"Smell that?" Mat breathed in the stench as if being a connoisseur of quality testing. He was pleased to savour the stench. "Books . . ., lots of books."

Tell gulped the foul air, detesting the staleness of heavy air. "You enjoy this smell?"

"I can't explain the sensation and the comforting meaning of the smell; as if the stronger the smell the better the quality of an aged living organism."

"Each to their own standard. Me, I would not eat fruit or meat that smelled as strongly as these decaying books."

Descending the circular stairwell, their body light began to illuminate deteriorating books piled randomly. Naked shelves containing sparse selections of books remaining in almost pristine condition invited touching. Mat gently brushed dust from covers and spines. Textures varied; bindings varied, and conditions seemed to span the scale of poor to poorer.

"These are old books." Mat's hands gently cradled a sample. "This is an archive. This book is leather bound; paper thick and very brittle with miniscule worm holes."

"For me, distasteful. For you it must be a succulent find."

"Yes, Yes." Mat gently placed the book onto the shelf making note of the title, 'Great Expectations'.

Tell's eyes darted from spine to spine and self to shelf. "We shall be here forever. I do not see a logical order to filing. There are numbers on each book and shelf, but I can not make sense of their meaning. And, titles are as random; 'Holy Bible, Training Dogs'. Maybe you could train Wojo to do some work. 'Fly fishing, Doctor Spock, Jake and the Kid by W.O. Mitchell'."

"What?"

"Jake and the Kid."

"No . . ., the Doctor book, it may be useful." Mat moved towards Tell, his eyes scanning the dust coated books.

"Here," Tell pointed. "A few of them; 'Doctor Spock – the Common-Sense book of Baby and Childcare, the First Two Years, a Better World for Our Children', and a few others."

"What, none on birthing?" Mat expressed disappointment, knowing that the odds would be against them finding a book immediately considering the vastness of the archive. Ninety percent of the room could not be seen beyond the reach of body light. "Take them."

"Which ones?"

"All of them. They may have merit."

Agreeing by shrugging shoulders, smirking and twitching whiskers, Tell began selecting copies with Doctor Spock's name on them. "One, two, three . . ., ten, eleven . . ., thirteen. Hey Mat, there must be a lot to know about babies and children."

"We won't need the information unless it is born . . . and survives."

Both men froze as the concept of birth, a foreign concept concerning humans, entered their thoughts. Visions of the calf births flashed bringing back anxiety and enthusiasm. If not for Sally's ability, surely a calf would have perished if left to nature's circumstances. In the moment of leaving the sustaining ability of the womb, the calf was dead. Sally intervened to jump-start life. For the calf life existed.

Occupants of the compound could not let the birth of a human take place as they stood by, inept, to witness complications of a still-birth. Sally held potential by using veterinary skills and adapting them to a human situation. Added support would be from the assembled residents of the compound. Without Mat and Tell providing a medical book, disaster would be devastating for all.

Legs and feet felt it first, a vibration of the structure beneath. Acute hearing picked up stress-pitched sounds of steel under tensile stress. Bracing themselves for support, the structure moved, the whole mountain of structure and earth shifted. Tell's blank stare to Mat questioned their current status. This was one of the largest rumbles of sound and shifting that Mat had experienced to date.

"Fairly normal," Mat intended to say with conviction, though his voice also rumbled sporadically.

"This is normal?" Expression of Tell's fear was the spiking of hair and bread, as if springs extended each hair with a puff of porcupine quills. "The earth moved!"

"Slightly more than normal."

"What is normal?" pleaded Tell, rushing to stuff the books into a sack while struggling to maintain an upright stance.

Normalcy would be an inert world. Earth lives and breaths internally and externally. During the current ice age, the exterior surface fluxed. Pressure of compression existed as the glaciers forced the earth's surface against man-made structures then against the mountain. Structural tension resisted compaction during the aggression of ice. With the retreat of the ice and flushing of debris by melting water, the fabricated structures began to relax and vent built-up tension.

"Normal will be the complete relaxation of all materials, man-made and organic."

Mat relaxed a grip on a shelf frame that did not seem to be secured. Rumbling and movement ceased, though sounds of creaking echoed from all directions.

"Without the pressure of the glacier forcing structures against the mountain, I expect the relaxation will allow everything to crumble . . ., sink . . ., as the bottom gives out."

"Mat?" Tell's word was calm in expression yet had a hint of expecting a definitive answer.

"Yes."

"When do you expect the disaster to occur?"

Mat paused tolerantly casual with emotion as the floor beneath their feet heaved as if the structure was taking a breath before sleep.

"Hundreds of years created this ice age and it will take an equal amount of time to recede. So . . ., I hope we find the medical book; head out, descend from the plateau, head to the compound, have a good meal and watch the mountain collapse from our rocking chairs when we are too old to complain." Mat smiled, an old framer's quizzical grin.

"Not reassuring to me, I'm already old." Closing the flap on the sack, Tell leaned against a wall with eagerness to exit. "Find the book and lets get out of here."

"How does this sound?" said Mat, a finger brushing dust from the spine of a book. "'Midwifery and Birthing through the Twentieth Century, Human Birthing Practice and Medical Care, Canadian Publication'?"

Tell inched towards the slanted staircase, his feet sensing the settling of the floor. "Sounds like a perfect book. The title covers everything; human birth and care. Not sure what 'Midwifery is', but we can find out when we get out of here."

Mat shrugged with compliance and retrieved the book as heavy dust dropped from the black void of the distant ceiling above. "This one also sounds good; 'Medical practice of birthing, Canadian Frontier 1800-1900'."

Reflecting from their body, light sparkled against the metallic composition of falling dust.

EIGHTEEN

"I don't care what people will think of me, nor what I do," May spittled through a mouthful of pickle juice as crunching sounds of a chewed pickle echoed. "This is a comfortable position."

While the compound residents gathered semi-circle around a prone body laying on the floor, Kat eyed the Mannerisms of the gathered. May rested on her back with legs bent up and spread wide. Residents were curious about the pregnant human; the only such person they had ever seen. Ocean birthing hosts were never viewed.

"Comfortable?" asked Sally casually, the only person to seem to be calm. Experience with animal births must require a calm demeanor.

"Yes, thank you. A bit of gurgling," May revealed, freely sharing all experiences. "Legs, belly and groin feel flabby."

Sally nodded then added an explanation by example, "As with bovine, prior to the actual birth, flesh and membranes relax and expand. May's flabby expression sums up what her body is doing to allow birth."

"Now!" Ed's voice jumped in pitch as eyes looked between May's spread legs.

"No, I am guessing a bit too early." Sally stood rigidly, keeping an eye on the plump belly for signs of May tightening muscles. "May seems too relaxed."

As if normal for the professors, always interested in gathering information, this anomaly of human reproduction held their inquisitiveness. In unison they leaned, crept closer with eyes wide and ears absorbing each detail Sally dictated. When encroachment began to invade privacy, Kat set down commands.

"Professors, please, though this must be of importance to all of us, a reasonable amount of decorum is required."

"Yes, yes, quite right," Pie said, stiffening a bent forward back. "We should not hover, bad for posture. Gather chairs around so we can sit to watch."

"No, no . . .!" Kat demanded, "Go away, do not hover. Go about, go clean and set up the domes for occupancy. We have new residents and need to arrange suitable occupancy."

As if scolded children, the professors reluctantly backed away and pretended to follow Kat's orders, though they accepted the demand as if only suggestions to be followed if whished. Pie, Phil, Story and even Ed backed away and wandered about the room, faking intent. While Kat and Sally catered to May's hunger and thirst, Jill and Art lingered in eye contact from opposite sides of May's sprawled body. Something about current circumstances developed odd thoughts in their minds, the stirring of spring emotions during a winter hibernation.

With the arrival of Tell and Sally, the professors, Jill, Ed and May, suitable accommodations were not finalized. Accommodating domes were available though had not been winterized and set up. Tell's dome and the professors' dome were used each year, yet each had added an additional body requiring space. The former dome once occupied by the seasonal doctor had not been used and gathered items of clutter. And, several other domes had been used for storage and as a hospital for sick animals. Good house keeping needed bodies to do the work. Kat glanced at the idle bodies occupying space.

"No meals until all domes are suitable for occupancy." Kat's formidable voice took charge. "Sally, I will take care of May. You can fix up Tell's dome as you see fit. Professors, fix up your dome. You need to make room for Art. It will be crowded, but the other domes will be needed for May, Ed and Jill."

With hands on hips expressing authority, her green eyes flashed a hint of dominance. "No meals!"

Fumbling to place their chairs correctly at the dinning table, the professors danced a path towards the door. Making sure May was comfortable, Sally followed the exiting crowd out into the afternoon calm.

"Ed, the first dome by this main dome is the cleanest and was set up as a hospital for sick livestock and next to Sally's dome for convenience."

Kat took Ed by the arm encouraging the man to leave and occupy thoughts on other matters. Disappointingly, he left when May smiled before crunching down on another pickle. In passing, Kat glanced at Jill's lively eyes staring at Art's bemused smile.

"Ed, don't come back until suppertime." Kat's hand had to force the man through the door opening.

Turning towards the centre of the room, Kat observed Jill and Art standing silently. An odd situation considering that the two had carried on a non-stop dialogue between themselves throughout the previous evening, in-spite of the combined chatter of the remaining group. She debated being too forward or offer a suggestive hint.

"Jill, Art?" Kat said, waving a hand between their line of sight.

"I know that look in Jill's eyes," May said before slurping a mouthful of juice. "She is quick to make decisions, and I think Art is an indecisive follower."

"That, he is," Kat agreed then raised her voice, "Time to get to work."

"Yes, I'm ready," answered Jill, staring down at May.

"Not on me. House keeping job first," May blurted.

Art awoke and stepped gently around May's tapping toes. He stood beside Jill, avoiding a study of the woman's intoxicating pattern of complexion patches.

Noticing that she had the attention of their eyes, Kat began offering suggestions, "The dome by the far path is a suitable accommodation for you Jill. Art, would you mind helping Jill. I do trust that the professors will make room for you in their dome. It has been crowded for the three of them, but they will squeeze you in . . ., maybe?"

"The crawler is crowded . . ., but I manage . . ., though I did sleep on the floor last night . . ., most inconvenient."

"Well . . ., that is too bad." A smile tinted Kat's facial feature. A knowing smile of a successful match-making tactic. "Jill will be comfortable once you take out all the junk. Room enough for two . . ., three . . ., though four people would be crowded."

"I see." Art's face sagged at the thought of a crowded dome with the other professors.

Opening the door, Kat ushered the two out. Jill's eyes were darting, as thoughts debated a synopsis. With head tilted forward, Art's puppy-dog form followed.

Jill's firm voice echoed back into the dome, "For the winter season . . ., I am open to a cohabitation contract. For as Kat said, the professors' dome is crowded."

Art stumbled, his head rising, peeking with interest.

"Jill is decisive," May said to the emptiness of the room.

"Another pickle?"

"Yes, please."

NINTEEN

Illumination began to fail on Mat and Tell's body lights just as they began to exit the excavation cave. A chilled air greeted them with a blast of reality. Winter's aggression had settled in with a breeze scraping across the plateau. Above, the heavens sparkled clear with every star twinkling through the crystalizing air. Nothing out of the ordinary for Mat, an all-season resident. The lateness of the evening worried Mat, for it would be a long descent from the plateau. Casting eyes out over the plain, the view provided a blanket of white hiding the lowlands. Only the peak of the beacon could be seen, a distant star among the backdrop of celestial stars.

"Where did the world go?" Tell exclaimed when viewing the thick blanket stretching in all directions. Only the top edge of the glacier remained in sight, its surface tinged by the Northern Borealis. "Which way is home?"

Mat pointed to the beacon. Without words of exclamation, he was contemplating a means of navigating home. In situations as this, he wished for the technologies of human's early abilities. A simple magnetic needle floating in a solution attracted to a specific earthly point would give bearings. An advanced satellite global positioning system would be pin-point accurate. Alas, earth's magnetic poles were no longer stable and useless for guidance. Satellites had fallen from orbits centuries earlier. Star guidance was an option here on the plateau with the heavens clear above. Once over the edge of the plateau they would be engulfed and secluded from all external objects.

"Good, the beacon . . .," Tell's panic subsided until realizing that the beacon was above the blanket of white. "Not so good once we are swallowed up by the dust of the snow storm."

"Quite right."

Mat turned to face in a three-hundred- and sixty-degree rotation to test directional wind. Eyes studied the swirling movements of the storm below. He faced the beacon and raised arms to a rough forty-five-degree angle on either side of the beacon to locate the brightest of star amongst star clusters. Satisfied that preliminaries of locations were registered, Mat quizzed Tell.

"Are you right handed or left, and which foot is your prominent in strength?"

Mat's face showed no indication of worry, as if the question was just inquisitive interest. Tell received the addressing with bewilderment. Why such nonsense when they were in a predicament. The compound was waiting for their return. What if circumstances had advanced beyond normal. He had faith in Sally's ability, yet she stressed the need for medical references. A delay by Mat's need of answers to trivial questions could mean disaster for May. Not only for the woman, but each person of the compound. Each individual is dependant on each other, and a whole sustains a singular entity. Tell wished to be an extension of this forthcoming new life. Devastation would be intolerable. The birth of bovine calves tingled every emotion never experienced before. What would a human birth do the senses? A frown twitched between eyebrows when questioning Mat's intent.

"Home . . ., we need to get home. And . . ., you ask irrelevant questions. I thought I knew you."

"You do. What you have to offer will help us get home. Bear with me."

Knowing that Mat had never mislead him, ever, throughout their acquaintance, Tell quickly answered and was prepared to do as instructed. "Left handed, foot, I don't know."

"Close your eyes and walk in place by lifting knees above each other."

Tell demonstrated until Mat said stop and opened eyes. When vision fell upon Mat, Tell's body had turned ten degrees to Mat's left. "Why did you move?"

"I didn't, your left foot is prominent, so you tend to veer to the right."

"Okay . . ., that clears matters up for me."

The explanation did not clear up any of Tell's confusion, though he remained silent and put all trust in Mat's abilities. Mat had technical matters arranged in his mind, and if followed, they would make it to the compound on a direct route.

"I have a strong right foot. We will walk side by side with you on my left. This will force us tp push against each other, thus keeping a straight tactical line. The storm is approaching the glacier from the south-west and will attack against our left cheek. Once the wind hits the face of the glacier it pushes down then begins to swirl back towards us at ground level. We should feel a cold against the back of our right leg."

Mat raised arms as before and faced the beacon. "If by chance through clear spots the bright stars in the clusters will be seen between our extended arms. We may be able to sight the beacon and if so, adjust direction onto our nose."

"Clear as mud. You do the guiding and I won't leave your side."

No further commentary was needed. Tell stepped beside Mat and they began to descend from the plateau into the bluster of white swirling snow. Without the aid of moonlight, the interior of the storm became a blackness void of physical objects. Loneliness hindered time. The pair had no indication of distance verses duration. Each step instant, yet advancement infinite.

May grunted from a position on the floor and all heads turned to gaze with anticipation of an unfolding problem. Only Sally had noticed a time lapse decreasing between grunts. Between mouths accepting the evening meal, conversations at the table would halt when May groaned. Held breaths waited then continued without breaking thoughts. Ed munched on an empty spoon pressed to lips. He could not take eyes away from May's movements. A shared amount of tension and physical manifestations were felt. Phantom pains gurgled in his stomach. Each professor grimaced when observing Ed's tormented face contort, mirroring every grunt echoing from the floor.

"Sorry Kat," May casually said between stomach pains. Her apology reaching Sally and Kat's ears at their place at the end of the table near her prone body. "I pee-ed a little."

"No big problem. It must be the excitement," Kat whispered, brushing off the incident until peering between May's spread legs. "Ohee . . ., a bit of a flood."

Kat's humorous words barely left smiling lips when May shrieked loud enough to send the house cat scrambling for a hiding place. Jill instinctively grasped Art's hand for emotional support. Though he winced, the touching was willingly accepted. Pie stepped from the table to pace, a means of calming nerves, though the intent did not help anyone. Story and Phil leaned towards Ed, his hands gripping the table.

"That is an unexpected plea!"

This was the first instant that Sally felt worried. Animals do not verbally react to pain with vocal sounds. The bovine breathed out heavily only after pushing the calf out. A relaxation sound after the strain of pushing. This sound indicated pain, and pain is usually an indication of a problem. "I am not ready even if this . . ., what do we call it, a calf, pup . . .?"

"A baby is the correct identification," offered Story.

"Yes, a baby." Sally retrieved a vet bag and opened it, unsure of what to reach for. "Where are Mat and Tell with a medical book?"

Rolling up sleeves, Sally began to disinfect hands. Thoughts began to compare procedures of birthing she had performed on various animals. May was a human, not an animal.

"Okay, back away. Everyone except Kat, back to the table. I think May would like a bit of privacy."

"We are professors, educators, reservoirs of learning. If we don't participate, or at least watch, how will we capture this miracle?" Pie said to all, expecting everyone to agree.

Phil shook his head no, while sliding to the far end of the table with a plate of food. Story withdrew a pad and pencil, willing to take notes instead of viewing.

"All back, I need room. If need be, I will give an explanation."

"Auh . . ., auh . . .! May's shriek interrupted Sally's words.

Something was happening. Sally had been counting the duration between pain spells and the length of each advancing scream. Less than a minute between a scream and May attempted to press hands against her large belly. While Kat draped a blanket over belly and bent knees, Sally began to remove May's lower garments. Suddenly, Pie became self conscious and retreated to the far end to mingle with the others. Eyes noticed Ed's facial colour varying in intensity of pink against a grey pigmentation. Slowly his head tilted and bobbed until he slumped against the table then slide onto the chairs. Eye-balls rolled; a belly heaved, arms circled above as if pulling required lifesaving air towards his mouth.

"Is Ed okay?" asked Phil.

"He is breathing," concluded Pie. "So, no need to worry."

"I feel faint," Story added.

"Keep your mind on taking notes, and breath deeply," Pie said, taking his own advice to swallow large gulps of air.

Art's fingers felt numb, yet he would not let himself pull away from Jill's grip. He wanted the affection, the sharing and the allure he had for this female. Private thoughts expressed the desire to be able to experience what May and Ed were having. Had evolution begun a change among landers, a new beginning, a continuation of existence on a rejuvenating land. Were thoughts realistic, after-all, he had just signed a winter seasonal cohabitation contract, and had not yet shared bedding with the female.

May's scream was freeing, not held back and vibrated throughout the dome. Goosebumps chilled onlookers. In the midst's of a scream the dome door burst open allowing cold air and snow to chill the internal warmth. Startled heads turned toward the black void of the opening. Breaths halted from breathing in the shivering cold air.

Side by side, Mat and Tell tried to force their way into the room. Shoulders compressed against each other and the door jams. Snowball heads hid the stiff features of the men. With arms locked together, they wobbled in, turned and forced the door closed. Shaggy-dog shaking reduced the accumulation of caked snow from their bodies. When turning back to face the residents, contorted faces searched for flexibility. Instantly minds realized that this situation in the dome was not right. Heads turned, and eyes noticed May laying and Sally and Kat in an intimate position. The others were a sorry looking bunch.

"I think May is calving," Tell managed to express through frozen lips.

"Yes . . ., and we have a medical book," Mat said twice, forcing the words louder on a second attempt.

Remaining locked in fixed arms, the pair plodded to the table. From their bags they dumped the collection of books.

"This is the medical book," pointed out Mat, attempting to open the book.

Slipping from stiff fingers, the book slammed against the table. Its brittle binding shattered allowing sectional portions of the stitched binding to scatter randomly. Lifting her head above the edge to peer down the length, Sally pleaded for quick assistance.

"Professors, take sections, read fast, read aloud important sections. Just read, do not interpret. I will decipher on the go. Start now!"

Hands grasped for sections, fingers and eyes scanning the ancient text on decomposing paper.

"Sally," Kat whispered. "May's groin is expanding just like the bovine."

"Hurry up professors," Sally's instructive voice did not vary, though internally, nerves, thoughts and anxiety were as frazzled as the others.

"Get this thing out of me. This is no fun," a low growl of a demon rumbled from May's throat.

"Professors?" Sally queried.

"Wash hands."

"Done"

"The cervix will dilate."

"The crown of the head should be visible with a membrane. This is the amniotic sack. If not broken, pinch, twist and break."

"Okay, I see, done, fluid expelled."

"Use hands, cup and guide."

TWENTY

A cry startled ears, a human cry, the first to be heard by any lander. A cry of birth in the compound dome witnessed by the guardians of a future generation. Only the cry reverberated stunning all into silence. Eyes looked up from the medical pages, staring towards the table end to watch Ed creep towards May, to lay beside. All waited anxiously to see the child that Sally and Kat fused over to bring to life. Tension stopped blood flow, stopped beating hearts and froze limbs in awkward poses.

Briefly, Sally raised the living form above the table edge. "This is a female, a true lander, our future."

United features and colouring integrated within all ocean humans molded this child's features. In one motion the watching gallery sighed and slumped into seats to mutter about their charge. Lowering the child to lay on May's belly and chest, Sally lifter her head above the table edge.

"We are not done, keep reading. I need to know about the umbilical chord, and care of the mother?"

"Here, I have it," Phil said. "This is work, I am hungry again." A finger found a place of importance. "Clamp the umbilical cord approximately a thumb's distance from the child's belly protrusion."

"Clean baby."

"Clear membrane, allow afterbirth to expel freely on its own." Story began, frowning at the technical aspects. "This is not the exciting part."

A change had come to the compound, a community of caregivers with a dedication to a miracle over odds that landers would be self-producing. Each day, evening, morning and even during nights, the baby would be passed from held arms to wanting arms. The essence of their lives was now the child, their future. Conversations debated the remembrance of the child's birth debate, care, upbringing and education. Doctor Spock's numbered books exchanged hands, were studied; suggestions applied, altered and discarded.

Conversations turned to the possibilities of Jill and Art's union and similar potential equal to what May and Ed were blessed with. As for the others, age and circumstances of the ocean induced sterility program, they resigned themselves to be the elder guardians. Community played a part in decisions to apply their trades. Sally stated she had to stay to doctor all animals and possible future human births.

Besides, Tell was deserving of staying in one place. As for the professors, they were desperately needed, they were the educators of a new lander generation. Art was a professor and had to stay to add his talents to the child's education. The truth was, he was attached to Jill, and she confirmed staying. And, art had signed Jill's cohabitation contract with an undefined end.

Kat braves the blowing wind and snow to follow Mat out to the centre of the compound. Weather slowly began clearing to allow sight of the star filled sky and dancing hues of the Northern Borealis. She survived the compound consisting of domes with lights of occupancy. A warm feeling satisfied thought of ever being alone again. She watched Mat cater to the beacon distributing its glow towards the outskirts of the plains.

"Are you expecting anyone else?"

"The survey crew told Ed they would return." Mat stared at the beacon then the expanse of the compound. "We exist, and others may arrive, thrive, and maybe bear children. Human existence may flourish despite the past flaws of humanity and earth's random need to deconstruct and rebirth."

EXISTENCE

OTHER TITLES AVAILABLE FROM
MOOSE HIDE BOOKS
Imprint of
MOOSE ENTERPRISE Publishing
Visit our web site at www.moosehidebooks.com for complete title
listings.

TITLES
      Steeltown
      Steeltown Blues
      Roosevelt Street
      Executor of Mercy
      A Print of a Man
      Sky Flyers
      Assault of a Princess
      Assault
      Basement Bargain Price Leafs For Sale
      Reflection
      Guilt in Accession
      Déjà vu
      Fragmentation of Life
      Dodger
      My Pecker Ain`t Working
      Cowboy Poetry for Sale
      Badland Trails
      Existence

www.ingramcontent.com/pod-product-compliance
Lightning Source LLC
Chambersburg PA
CBHW031835170626
46807CB00004B/1464